PUFFIN BOOKS

PRIMEVAL

FIGHT FOR SURVIVAL

PRIMEVAL
FIGHT FOR SURVIVAL

Adapted by Alicia Brodersen

PUFFIN

PUFFIN BOOKS

Published by the Penguin Group
Penguin Books Ltd, 80 Strand, London WC2R ORL, England
Penguin Group (USA) Inc., 375 Hudson Street, New York, New York 10014, USA
Penguin Group (Canada), 90 Eglinton Avenue East, Suite 700, Toronto, Ontario, Canada M4P 2Y3
(a division of Pearson Penguin Canada Inc.)
Penguin Ireland, 25 St Stephen's Green, Dublin 2, Ireland (a division of Penguin Books Ltd)
Penguin Group (Australia), 250 Camberwell Road, Camberwell, Victoria 3124, Australia
(a division of Pearson Australia Group Pty Ltd)
Penguin Books India Pvt Ltd, 11 Community Centre, Panchsheel Park, New Delhi – 110 017, India
Penguin Group (NZ), 67 Apollo Drive, Rosedale, North Shore 0632, New Zealand
(a division of Pearson New Zealand Ltd)
Penguin Books (South Africa) (Pty) Ltd, 24 Sturdee Avenue, Rosebank,
Johannesburg 2196, South Africa

Penguin Books Ltd, Registered Offices: 80 Strand, London WC2R ORL, England

puffinbooks.com

First published 2008
I

Set in Times New Roman
Typeset by Palimpsest Book Production Limited, Grangemouth, Stirlingshire
Made and printed in England by Clays Ltd, St Ives plc

British Library Cataloguing in Publication Data
A CIP catalogue record for this book is available from the British Library

ISBN: 978-0-141-32394-7

FIGHT FOR SURVIVAL

It was coming to the end of a long, dull day at the Castle Cross shopping centre for Barry Somerville. The burly security guard had spent his shift catching a petty thief nicking crisps in the food court, cautioning three wannabe rappers for break-dancing inside the electronics store and wasted half the afternoon trying to find balls that had gone missing from the bowling alley.

Barry sighed as he did his final round of the now empty complex. So much for the '*So you think you're James Bond?*' blurb on the job advert he'd read all those years ago. He'd been a guard at the shopping centre for nearly a decade, and he hadn't been sent on a secret spy mission once.

At least his shift was nearly over. Barry walked into the security office and nodded a greeting to Graham, a younger guard who was finishing off some paperwork. Pulling out a Thermos full of coffee from his locker,

Barry settled in front of the CCTV monitors to check everything was in order. He was already thinking about the pizza he was going to pick up on his way home.

Barry frowned as the image of the bowling alley flickered on to the screen. Calling Graham over, the two security guards watched as a ball came tumbling down one of the long, polished wooden laneways in the wrong direction. As the camera flicked to another section of the entertainment quarter, Barry put on his security belt and headed for the door. Even though it didn't look like there was anyone down there, he had to check it out just the same. The ball couldn't have come from just *nowhere*. Someone was clearly having a laugh.

As Graham kept watch on the screens upstairs, Barry stepped into the deserted bowling alley. The harsh neon lights illuminated a dozen polished laneways, and the only noise was the gentle whirring of a slushie machine. Barry wondered if he could get away with grabbing a quick drink while he was down here. He could always pay for it tomorrow.

The security guard's thoughts were interrupted by the sound of something slithering along the small corridor that ran the length of the alleyway, behind the pins. Without warning, the loud sound of wood splintering echoed around the centre. A snapped skittle landed at Barry's feet.

Annoyed, Barry walked down the laneway, crouching as he reached the end to inspect the remaining ninepins. From the harsh light in the alley above him, he could just discern the outline of someone squeezed into the shadows of the pin deck.

'All right,' Barry groaned, getting frustrated now. 'Fun's over!'

The person didn't move. Barry rolled his eyes – trust him to get a stupid kid wanting to play games at the end of his shift!

'I need backup,' the security guard said into his walkie-talkie, hoping to scare the youth into coming out. 'We have an intruder.'

Barry inched closer to the pin deck as he remembered the problems at the alley earlier today. Several players had reported that their balls had disappeared down the laneways, instead of coming back up through the electronic ball return like they were supposed to. The management had checked all their equipment but couldn't find any faults with it. It was pretty obvious someone had been nicking them.

Barry was becoming increasingly convinced he'd finally found the troublemakers.

'Don't make me come in there and get you!' he shouted, inching closer to the pin deck.

Barry made a quick lunge forward, trying to grab at the person in the shadows. But as he did, the figure moved. Barry grappled for his torch, shining it at the figure.

He couldn't believe what he saw.

Whatever it was, it certainly wasn't a human – it didn't even look like any animal he knew, either. Instead, Barry could see what appeared to be a reptile of some sort, with a thick, leathery body, standing as tall as a human on its muscular hind legs. It had tiny, clawed arms protruding from halfway up its stomach, and a huge mouth filled with rows of sharp teeth.

And it was coming straight for him.

Barry screamed as the creature suddenly sprang from its hiding place in the shadows. Grabbing hold of the terrified guard's arm, its teeth easily sliced through the thick security jacket as it quickly began pulling Barry back into the pin deck. Unable to get a grip on the shiny, polished floorboards or the gutter, the guard had no chance.

Moments later, Graham arrived out of breath to find the bowling alley empty. The last thing he'd seen on the security screen was Barry crouching down, calling for backup.

Graham's eyes widened as a ball suddenly spat out of the pin deck at the opposite end of one of the laneways. As he walked over for a closer inspection, his mouth became dry with fright.

Running behind the ball was a wet trail of red. As Graham squinted at the ball, he noticed that it was dark with blood. And Barry was nowhere to be seen.

CHAPTER 2

Although they'd never met each other, the lives of Professor Nick Cutter and Barry Somerville were about to become inextricably linked. Granted, Nick Cutter was not about to be killed by a vicious reptilian creature today, but his afternoon was turning out to be nearly as bad as Barry's.

In fact, standing in front of a glittering cluster of light, or an 'anomaly', in the Forest of Dean, Cutter was having the worst day of his life.

He'd often called anomalies 'ruptures in time' – rips in the atmosphere. Since they had been appearing, prehistoric creatures had stumbled across them and blundered through from the past to the present, and it was up to Cutter and his team to contain the intruders and prevent havoc. But it also meant that humans could travel through these tears in time. As Cutter had done – he had just returned from the Permian era, which was 250 million years ago . . .

But as Cutter had walked back into the present, here in the Forest of Dean, his world had turned on its head. And right now, he was feeling completely bewildered and disorientated. This wasn't the world he had left behind when he stepped through the anomaly into the Permian era just hours ago. Somehow, while he was gone, the woman he loved had been erased from history.

It had begun as any other normal day – well, normal for Cutter, anyway. A palaeontologist from the Central Metropolitan University, he'd recently been studying the phenomenon of anomalies. Together with his lab assistant, Stephen Hart, graduate student Connor Temple and zoologist Abby Maitland, the small team had been discovering and exploring these unusual occurrences in areas across southern England.

The anomalies had been appearing for several months now and were easily identifiable. Usually a few metres wide and several metres high, they hovered in the air like bright circles of light, crystal-like shards glowing from their edges.

Occasionally, harmless creatures came through – like the playful dinosaur lizard Coelurosauravus, one of which Abby had adopted as a pet. Or the majestic flying Pteranodon, which had been safely returned to

9

the past almost a week ago. But more often than not, the creatures were deadly predators who, if let loose on the modern world, would cause death and devastation. They already had a flock of flying Pterosaurs, who stripped the flesh off their victims in minutes, and a deadly giant centipede, which had nearly killed Stephen with its lethal bite.

Apart from Nick and his team, there were only a handful of people who knew the whole truth about these strange happenings. The first was Helen Cutter – another palaeontologist and Nick Cutter's estranged wife. They weren't a couple any more. After all, Helen had chosen to disappear for eight years, hiding in the anomalies and exploring the wonders of the past. And while she was gone, Cutter gradually lost hope, finally coming to the conclusion she was dead. She'd only recently come back to the present because she was forced to. And even though Helen refused to tell them how, she was the only one who knew how to detect anomalies before they opened.

Two other people who knew about the anomalies were James Lester, a government crony who worked for the prime minister, and Claudia Brown, a representative from the Home Office. They'd both been put in charge to keep an eye on the team and make sure reports of dinosaur appearances weren't leaked to the general public.

But a few days back, an even more sinister creature had arrived, one which none of them had been expecting – or even thought possible. It had come from an anomaly hidden in the Permian era that led not to the past, but to the *future*. After the discovery of the predator's offspring and the death of the male adult creature, Cutter had been put in charge of returning the futuristic babies to their proper place in time.

Earlier this afternoon, he and Helen and several soldiers from the SAS had stepped through an anomaly in the Forest of Dean and into the Permian era, carrying the crate containing the grotesque, squealing infants. But disaster had struck not long after they'd made camp – a female Future Predator had followed and attacked them, killing all the soldiers and their commanding officer Captain Ryan. If it hadn't been for a hungry Gorgonopsid crushing the creature to death and eating its young, the Future Predator would have killed them too.

Just minutes ago, Cutter and Helen had finally come back through the anomaly to tell everyone the dreadful news. Captain Ryan and all the SAS soldiers were dead. But as far as they knew, all the Future Predators and their babies had also perished. Cutter had quickly told his gathered team, Lester and the remaining SAS soldiers that no one should ever go through into the past again. But as always, Helen had other ideas. She'd tried to entice Stephen to come back with her to continue explorations in the Permian era and try to find the anomaly that led to the future. When Stephen refused, Helen had stormed off through the anomaly, furious.

As the sun had begun to set, Cutter stood in the tranquil Forest of Dean, trying to make sense of it all. It had been a terrifying and bewildering afternoon. But he knew that at least he had Claudia to rely on. The two of them had become quite close, even sharing a kiss before Cutter had left just hours ago. Cutter had looked around trying to find her among the gathered faces, knowing that he could rely on her to make him feel better.

But Claudia hadn't been there. And when Cutter asked where she was, the rest of the group had shaken their heads, adamant that they didn't know who he was talking about.

And now . . . Cutter's head spun with confusion. Even grabbing Claudia's haughty boss, James Lester, and shouting into his smug face had done no good

– even *Connor* backed up what Lester was saying! Cutter felt like he was going to be violently ill. Something they'd done in the past had affected the present and as a result, Claudia was missing. It was as if she'd never been born.

Cutter whirled round to face the anomaly shining behind him, convinced the only way to find Claudia would be to go back through. The light had been glimmering brilliantly when he and Helen returned, but now it was beginning to fade. Cutter's heart sank. The anomaly that had been open for months was about to close!

Cutter lunged forward, throwing himself towards the light.

'Don't be stupid!' Stephen shouted, grabbing hold of the professor's arm and pulling him back. 'You could be marooned there forever!'

'I have to go!' Cutter cried, trying desperately to loosen the lab technician's grip. 'I have to make things right!'

But it was too late. As Cutter watched helplessly, the beams shimmered for one final second before dissolving into thin air. And any hope of finding Claudia had just disappeared with it.

CHAPTER 3

Lester had been watching Nick Cutter with a mix of fear, loathing and fascination. In his mid-thirties, with messy blond hair and wearing a dusty khaki jacket and jeans, Cutter wasn't the typical image of a stuffy old professor. But after working with him over the course of the last few months, Lester was starting to suspect Cutter was unstable. And the fact that he had now come back through an anomaly ranting about someone that Lester had never even *heard* of going missing, made him even more certain. The man had clearly cracked.

Lester's thoughts were interrupted by his mobile phone ringing. He was being called to an urgent meeting at the office.

'I think we're done here, aren't we?' he asked briskly, brushing imaginary specks of dust from his lapels and striding off towards his car without waiting for an answer.

Cutter rushed after him. He knew Lester despised him, but he had to make him understand. He just *had* to find Claudia.

'Claudia Brown was in charge of the day-to-day anomaly operation,' Cutter said urgently, grabbing a surprised Lester by the arm. 'She's been with us since the beginning!'

'No,' Lester said, shaking Cutter off like a particularly irritating fly. 'That's Leek.'

Lester's eyes narrowed as a wave of incomprehension swept over Cutter's face. Was the professor deranged, or just being obstinate?

'Oliver Leek,' he added slowly, not hiding the fact that he thought Cutter was a fool. 'You can't have forgotten him. You saw him at the ARC this morning.'

'The what?' said Cutter, frowning.

Lester sighed audibly as Abby came to stand beside them. She could tell Cutter wasn't himself and wondered if the stress from the shocking events inside the Permian anomaly was getting to him. Maybe later she'd suggest he go home to get some rest.

'The ARC . . .' she explained helpfully, urging him to remember. 'The Anomaly Research Centre.'

'You mean the Home Office?' Cutter replied. This

was all getting too confusing. The Home Office was what they'd always used as their base when it came to discussing the anomalies. He'd never heard of the ARC before – it certainly hadn't existed when he'd gone into the Forest of Dean this afternoon.

Abby shook her head, trying to smile. Cutter could tell by her quizzical look that she thought he had concussion or something.

'No,' she said, her pretty face looking at him kindly. 'We moved to a new place ages ago.'

'Is he having a nervous breakdown?' Lester interrupted, curling his top lip and talking to no one in particular. 'Only, I've got a meeting, so if someone could just call an ambulance.'

'He's fine,' Abby said, taking hold of Cutter's arm protectively. It wouldn't do to let Lester think he had the upper hand. His stiff government protocol made things difficult enough for the team as it was.

Lester stared at the two of them before rolling his eyes towards the sky. He'd really had enough of these simpletons and their dinosaur hoo-ha today. If Cutter *was* finally losing it, it wasn't his problem. Still, it wouldn't hurt to humour the professor a little bit.

'This Claudia Brown,' Lester said, getting into the

back of his government car and feigning interest. 'Was she anyone important, or just a member of the public?'

Cutter fixed him with a steely glare. Unconcerned, Lester quickly shut his door and waved at the driver to leave.

Little did Cutter know that it wouldn't be long before he was able to see the Anomaly Research Centre for himself. The team had received a message – one of the operators at the ARC had intercepted an emergency call from a young security guard named Graham at the Castle Cross shopping mall. He'd been screaming about being attacked by 'some kind of monster' – the last radio communication anyone had had from him. The ARC thought it important enough to warrant a proper investigation.

After driving there with Abby, Stephen and Connor, Cutter now stood on the top floor of the split-level centre, utterly transfixed. He'd never seen anything like it. Masses of high-tech equipment dotted the enormous room – a large electronic map of the UK loomed over a lower floor manned by dozens of surveillance and support staff, pinpointing areas of interest. Cutter recognized several dots on the map highlighting anomalies they'd discovered over the course of the last few months. The operation's sheer size was a long way from the small meeting rooms they'd occupied at the Home Office.

'Glad to see you're back safe and well, Professor,' said a man in an expensive business suit, sidling up to Cutter with familiarity. 'But I gather your wife won't be joining us?'

Cutter drew his eyes from the vast room to inspect the government operative in front of him. He was in his early thirties, not much older than Stephen, and his seemingly permanent smirk gave him an air of someone who couldn't be trusted. Cutter had never seen him before in his life.

'Who on earth are you?' he said, frowning.

'Professor Cutter is suffering some kind of stress-related amnesia,' Lester cut in, talking over the man's shoulder. 'He seems to have forgotten, well, pretty much *everything*, really.'

'I haven't forgotten a thing!' Cutter protested, annoyed at Lester behaving as if he wasn't there. 'I wish I could!'

'And now he's being enigmatic as well,' sighed Lester mockingly, still speaking to the man in front of them. 'What a vivid repertoire.' The government official looked pityingly at Cutter. 'Are you *really* telling me you don't know who this man is?'

Cutter stared at Lester blankly. What game was he playing? It was obvious he didn't believe him – but no one did, for that matter. If Claudia wasn't around to fight in their corner any more, who knew what silly excuse Lester would find to get rid of the whole team. He could do whatever he wanted with the anomalies, and any dinosaurs that came through them – a move that could prove disastrous for humankind. And if Cutter appeared to be no longer useful, Lester would be itching to have him thrown out at the first available opportunity.

Cutter groaned inwardly. The only way he was going to *find* Claudia was if he still had access to the anomalies and the ARC's resources. He'd have to amuse Lester until he could figure out exactly what was going on.

Cutter flashed Lester a winning smile. He genuinely had no idea who this person in front of him was, but he was going to have to take a stab. Claudia's life depended on it.

'Of course I do!' he said, remembering the name Lester had dropped earlier. 'You're Oliver Leek.'

Leek looked at Cutter uncertainly, not seeming

entirely convinced. Lester, meanwhile, was busy sneering at Abby, Connor and Stephen, who had been watching the conversation with interest.

'Is this some kind of industrial action?' he said, clapping his hands as if herding sheep. 'Or did none of you hear we have a creature sighting in a shopping mall?'

'We're on our way,' said Stephen, leading the team into the storage area. Cutter found himself shaking his head again. Since when had they allowed Lester to push them around? And where had all this flashy equipment come from? Cutter looked at the storage facility, impressed. Rucksacks, camping equipment, oxygen tanks and several pieces of serious-looking firearms lined the walls. Abby, Connor and Stephen began kitting themselves up, obviously familiar with the process. Cutter grabbed what he could as the others made their way out of the door.

Hurrying down a hallway towards the car park, Connor pulled back. He hadn't had a chance to talk to the professor since he'd returned from the anomaly, and he had plenty of unanswered questions.

'You didn't have a clue who Leek was, did you?' he said quietly, as Abby and Stephen ran ahead.

As much as he felt the need to lie to Lester, Cutter

knew he couldn't lie to his team. What was the point, anyway? He looked at Connor and shook his head.

'You're really beginning to freak me out. You're saying something's changed because of what happened in the Permian anomaly? That evolution has altered course?'

Cutter allowed himself a half smile as he looked over at the scruffy student. If it hadn't been for Connor coming to him about the very first dinosaur sighting, they would never have discovered the initial anomaly in the Forest of Dean all those months ago. Connor might have got himself into plenty of trouble along the way, but his heart was usually in the right place. If he was willing to believe the professor now, then Cutter could really do with an ally.

'I'm glad someone was listening,' he replied finally.

'OK,' said Connor, considering things carefully. After all, he loved conspiracy theories and he'd seen plenty of weird things since the anomalies opened up. Who was to say the professor wasn't telling the truth? 'I'll buy it.'

'You believe me?' Cutter asked incredulously.

'You've never been wrong before,' Connor replied, as Cutter looked like he was about to hug him.

'Connor,' he said happily, his thick Scottish accent breaking up. 'I could kiss you!'

Connor stopped dead in his tracks. *This* wasn't normal. Cutter usually wanted to yell at him for something – not snog him.

'I'd rather you didn't,' Connor said, noticing Abby talking to Stephen down at the end of the corridor. Connor and Abby were flatmates and he'd had the biggest crush on her forever. 'Well, not now. But just one more thing,' Connor pulled his messy, shoulder-length hair behind his ears nervously. 'How do I know how I'm different when I don't know what I was like before?'

'Don't worry,' Cutter laughed, reading Connor's thoughts about the pretty young zoologist as they finally reached the car park. 'Some people never change!'

Abby and Stephen stood outside the shopping centre, filling tranquillizer darts underneath the light of a street lamp. Abby could only guess the dosage – they had no idea what size creature they were dealing with. She knew they could never guess what kind of dinosaur to expect from an anomaly. They'd had everything from twenty-kilogram Dodos to a one-tonne Scutosaurus come through.

'Can I have a gun?' Connor asked eagerly. The bemused look on Stephen's face said it all. No.

'Abby's got one,' he protested.

'She knows how to use it,' the handsome laboratory assistant pointed out, as Abby loaded the rifle.

'How many animals have *you* tranquillized?' Abby added sarcastically, already knowing the answer.

Connor scowled. He didn't like it when people ganged up on him. Especially when it was these two. He knew Abby really liked Stephen, and Connor was beginning to wonder whether she was always going to see him as just a friend and her flatmate, and nothing more. Connor didn't want to admit it to himself.

'I've played darts!' he said defensively. 'How hard can it be to hit a giant predator from a few metres?' His protest was met with a deafening silence. Connor sulked. 'Sometimes I think you don't trust me with firearms.'

'Whatever gives you that idea?' Stephen grinned as Cutter stepped into the lamplight. He turned to the professor. 'So. What do we do now?'

'We go in,' he suggested, lifting up a pack and heading towards the brightly lit entrance of the Castle Cross shopping centre.

A shutter was pulled down over the front door. But before they could discuss how to get inside, they heard a sharp scraping noise moving behind the barricade. Abby's heart skipped a beat as she raised her rifle, knowing how easily an angry dinosaur could destroy such a flimsy object.

Without warning, the shutter flew up and open.

A pale-looking man was standing there, holding his hands up in surrender. He'd had a tense evening, and the last thing he needed was three people pointing large weapons at him. Stephen flipped open his ID as the man explained he was the duty manager at the mall. Cutter was curious about the last thing they'd heard from Graham the security guard.

'He didn't really *say* anything,' the duty manager stuttered, looking forward to getting home and having a cup of tea. 'He just sort of . . . screamed.'

'Open the door,' Cutter instructed, having no time for niceties. The duty manager did as he was told with a look of relief. If someone else was willing to go in there and sort this out, that was fine by him. 'Lock the doors behind us and keep them locked until I tell you it's safe. Whatever happens, it mustn't get out.'

'*What* mustn't get out?' the man asked, looking up from the keys in his hands. But Cutter, Stephen, Abby and Connor were already on their way inside. The duty manager fumbled with the lock and gratefully ran over to the safety of his car. He didn't want to stay out here any longer than he had to.

Minutes later, the team were in the security office, watching the CCTV images Barry and then Graham had spotted earlier that afternoon. There was a tense atmosphere in the room.

Right now, though, they'd come to the part of the tape that Graham had missed as he ran down to the bowling alley. Barry was crouching down, shining a torch into the pin deck. Seconds later, *something* dragged him along the ground as he struggled helplessly.

'Can you get any closer?' Cutter asked, as Connor tried to zoom in on the picture. There was a stunned silence as the image of Graham watching the bowling ball roll back up the laneway came on to the screen. Seconds later, a large creature walked past the camera behind him. Just as Graham turned in horror, Connor froze the picture. Unable to stop himself, Cutter let out an appreciative gasp.

'A Cretaceous-era Theropod dinosaur,' he murmured excitedly. 'The genuine article.'

'Some species of Raptor,' Connor added, nodding. 'I always hoped we'd get one some day.'

'Beautiful . . .' the scientist whispered, trying to zoom in on the vicious carnivore. Before he was brought into the anomaly project, he never would have guessed he'd be able to see a living, breathing Raptor up close. But it wasn't long before Cutter realized the rest of the team was looking at him curiously. 'I said it was beautiful,' he qualified, studying the creature's razor-sharp teeth on the screen with fascination. 'I didn't say it was friendly!'

The group made their way down to the bowling alley as Cutter instructed them to branch out and search for the anomaly. If this was where the creature had been, there was no doubt the atmospheric rip would be close by.

It didn't take them long to find it. Shimmering brightly, the large circle of light glimmered invitingly from the last lane at the far end of the centre. The group clamoured around the glowing light, ducking out of the way as the magnetic pull of the anomaly sent a metal chair flying past them and into the light.

'Maybe the Raptors have gone back?' Connor asked hopefully.

Cutter looked at him ruefully. If only life was that simple. Cutter realized if the creature wasn't here, then they would have to go looking for it. Instructing Abby and Connor to inspect the food court, he and Stephen made their way out of the bowling alley and towards the atrium in the centre of the mall.

CHAPTER 5

Less than half an hour later, Stephen and Cutter were alerted by Abby and Connor shouting from another area of the mall. As they raced towards the food court, they could see Abby urgently pushing against a button beside a closing partition, desperately trying to close the shutter as fast as possible. She was yelling at a terrified Connor, who was belting towards her at full speed. Behind the frantic student, Cutter could see the very real and awe-inspiring sight of a fearsome Utahraptor.

The creature was magnificent in its fury, and for a terrible second, the professor wondered how on earth Connor was going to outrun it. With the length of its body and tail, the Raptor was over five metres long and taller than he was. Its long, thin forearms were attempting to reach out and grasp Connor as he wove among tables and chairs trying to disorientate it. Cutter knew if the creature managed to grab hold of Connor with its taloned claws, it would then pull him down and kick him with its powerful hind legs – a move that could prove deadly. With a huge, curved claw on each foot, all it had to do was slash at Connor's throat and then –

A wave of relief washed over the professor as he realized Connor was going to make it. With centimetres to spare, the student slid underneath the shutter just as it was about to close. Behind him, the angry Utahraptor battered against the partition, still determined to claim its prey. It was a good few minutes before it gave up, and the team heard it move off to another area of the shopping centre behind them.

'We need more firepower,' Stephen decided as Abby and Connor caught their breath. The tranquillizer darts they had prepared had nowhere near enough dosage to bring down a creature of that size and strength.

But Cutter shook his head. It was probably killing the Future Predators that had caused Claudia to disappear. As far as he was concerned, it would only cause them problems if more creatures ended up dead.

'I've lost a friend because we played games with

nature once too often,' he said, shaking his head. 'I don't intend to let it happen again.'

Stephen looked at Cutter dubiously. Together they'd spent years researching various fossil and palaeontology finds and they knew each other well. Stephen was concerned that Cutter was talking about this Claudia Brown so much, he actually thought she had existed. It wasn't like the professor to be so scatty.

Anyway, there wasn't time to think about that now – the team had to move on. As they headed along a walkway, a skimming sound echoed around the corner. Readying his gun and putting his finger to his lips, Cutter motioned Abby and Stephen to come beside him and together the three of them burst into the open space of the atrium.

But it wasn't a Raptor that confronted them. Instead, a startled cleaner on an electric polisher stared at them wide-eyed with surprise.

'Don't shoot!' the man begged, holding his hands up.

Stephen couldn't stop himself from laughing with relief as he asked Abby and Connor to take the man outside. The cleaner said he hadn't seen a thing, which was just as well. They didn't know how they'd explain a five-metre-long Raptor on the loose.

Back at the ARC, Lester had just finished looking at photos of the shopping centre before placing a call to Stephen. Cutter had confirmed there was an anomaly and yet another random man-eater on the loose. Not for the first time, Lester wondered whether his overtime was really worth all this hassle.

'I'll put armed backup on standby and tell the owners there's a security scare,' Lester said, finishing off the conversation. 'They'll have to stay closed for as long as it takes.'

Hanging up the phone, he cringed as a printed email was thrust in his face.

'Leek,' he said, with a withering look, 'has the concept of personal space ever been explained to you?'

'Sorry, sir,' Leek replied, taking a step back. 'But it's from the minister, marked "Top Priority".'

Lester groaned and took the page, reading over it quickly.

'A private sector public relations manager?' he said, raising his voice a couple of octaves. 'What am I supposed to do with one of those?'

'The minister thinks we need more help with the media,' Leek replied, with an air of superiority. 'He feels the situation is getting out of hand.'

Lester glared at the younger man. Who was Leek to tell him how to handle things? That lunatic Cutter and his three potty sidekicks were chasing a giant prehistoric creature through the local shopping centre with state-of-the-art bazookas right now, and Lester had up-to-the-minute updates. The situation looked perfectly under control from where he was standing.

'His words, sir,' added Leek, reading Lester's thoughts. 'Not mine.'

Lester frowned. The last thing he needed was some greasy PR supremo sucking up to the press. It wasn't a reality TV show. Still, if word of this got out, no one would ever go to Castle Cross to do their shopping again. It would go bust for sure. How was he supposed to explain *that* to the mall's owners?

'Maybe a PR person isn't such a bad idea after all,' he sighed, waving Leek away to write a reply to the minister.

Lester turned back to the group of photos he'd been studying before Leek had arrived. Flicking through various shots of the Castle Cross shopping centre, he stopped when he came to the one of the cleaners' storerooms. Straightening the rest of the pictures, he put it on the top of the pile and promptly tried to forget all about Castle Cross. Cutter and his team would take care of it.

CHAPTER 6

Abby and Connor ushered the cleaner through the back corridors of the mall, towards the staff locker rooms. The man was adamant that he needed his wallet and keys if he was going to be able to get home. Abby and Connor couldn't help but agree with him.

Still, something was wrong as they got closer to the room. They could see the door was ajar. Abby frowned.

'Did you leave that door open?' she said, eyeing it with caution.

'I don't remember,' the cleaner said vaguely. He looked like he just wanted to get out of there. Connor saw them both hesitate and took his chance.

'Give me the gun,' he said, motioning to the weapon Abby was holding.

'What?' she spluttered, amazed that he'd even dare ask. 'No!'

'Oh, come on!' Connor wheedled, noticing she

hadn't taken any steps closer towards the door. 'Just for a minute. Do *you* want to go first?'

Abby pouted. Of *course* she didn't. As far as she was concerned, if there was a flesh-eating predator behind the door, she was happy for *anyone* to go ahead of her. Reluctantly, she handed the gun to Connor.

'Thought not,' he said. Pulling his shoulders back, Connor flashed Abby with what he thought was a devilish grin. Did she ever look cute – even when she was scared! With her short blonde hair and tomboy style, she was kind of like a hipper, modern-day Lara Croft. But anyway, Connor didn't have time to think about that. He had the world to save.

Connor kicked open the door and burst into the room, spinning around like one of Lester's SAS soldiers. He turned and nodded to Abby and the cleaner.

'Clear!' he shouted, stating the obvious.

Abby rolled her eyes as the cleaner walked over to his locker and Connor waved the gun about, making firing noises with his mouth. He could be such a loser sometimes!

But Connor wasn't pretending for long. Without warning the cleaner screamed, as Abby and Connor saw an infant Raptor leap out of the locker and clamp its jaws round the hapless mall-worker's neck.

Although it was less than a metre long, the creature's razor-sharp teeth sliced viciously at his skin as it screeched furiously. Connor stood frozen to the spot in horror.

'Do something!' Abby yelled, pointing at the gun he'd been waving around just seconds before.

Connor was petrified. He'd never used a *real* gun before. With shaking hands, he levelled it at the Raptor, trying to aim properly as the creature and the cleaner flailed about the room. Shooting off the first dart, he was horrified to watch it sail through the air and connect perfectly with Abby's thigh. Without time to think, he reloaded the gun as the cleaner and Raptor crashed to the ground. Running over and kicking the creature away, Connor fired a dart at it at point-blank range. The dinosaur bared its teeth at him before wobbling for a second and falling over, temporarily out cold.

Connor bent down to check on the injured cleaner. His neck was bleeding pretty badly, but at least he was alive. He turned to check on Abby. She glared at him accusingly as she leant helplessly against the wall, half sitting, half standing. She was tugging feebly at the dart in her leg.

'You . . . *idiot* . . .' she slurred, as her eyes rolled

back in her head and she slowly slid down to the floor and passed out.

Connor looked around in dismay. One cleaner, one baby Raptor and one potential girlfriend were all lying at his feet. And not a single one of them conscious!

Elsewhere in the shopping centre, Stephen and Cutter had just brought down a Raptor of their own. Swiftly tracking the large adult through the amusement arcade and then the hi-fi section of a department store, they'd finally sent it hurtling to the ground with a heavily laden dart in the women's clothes section. Judging by its size, this was possibly the same Utahraptor that had attacked Abby and Connor in the food court.

But they had to decide what to do quickly. They both knew Abby had guessed the dosage of the dart – there was no way to tell how long they had before it woke up again.

'Look at it,' Cutter sighed, stopping for a moment. No matter how many dinosaurs he'd been chased by these last few months, he was still in awe of every one of them. He and Stephen had spent their whole careers studying fossils and bones. To have the opportunity to see a real live creature was something else. 'The perfect killing machine,' he added, crouching down to inspect the Raptor's brilliant blue head crest. 'In a fair fight we mammals wouldn't stand a chance.'

'Speaking as a mammal,' Stephen chuckled, 'I'm all in favour of cheating.'

For a moment, it felt like old times. Cutter looked up at Stephen, wondering if now was the time to discuss what had happened at the anomaly this afternoon. After all, they'd been friends for a long while and Stephen had known Helen before her disappearance eight years ago as well. But when she'd asked him to go back with her into the Permian era, she'd also revealed to everyone that the two of them had once been more than just friends. Cutter had no idea about it, and as Helen had hoped, he had been shocked. But he didn't want to lose his long friendship with Stephen over it.

'Listen,' the professor said, taking a deep breath. 'You could have gone with Helen, but you didn't. Right now, that's all that matters. The rest is history.'

Stephen ran his hand through his dark brown hair nervously. Cutter was right – anything that had happened between him and Helen was in the past. If Cutter was willing to leave it at that for the moment, then so was he.

'Do you think she'll be back?' he replied finally.

'You mean has she finished messing with us yet?' Cutter wondered, remembering Helen's face as she'd watched him kissing Claudia in the Forest of Dean. She hadn't been happy. 'I seriously doubt it. Helen never handled rejection very well.'

Suddenly, their conversation was interrupted by Connor's shouts. It sounded as though he was over by the atrium. Quickly binding the dozing Raptor, they ran towards the noise.

Over by the lifts, they were shocked to come across Connor impatiently hopping from one foot to the other, a knocked-out Abby lying at his feet, since he had carried her there from the locker room.

'What *happened*?' Cutter asked, kneeling down beside Abby.

'I shot her,' Connor said as Cutter and Stephen stared at him. He realized how ridiculous it sounded. 'It was collateral damage!' he protested. 'I got the Raptor too.'

'You brought down a full-size Raptor on your own?' Cutter asked, his jaw dropping in disbelief.

'Well, *nearly* full size,' Connor replied, not wanting to admit the creature was just a baby. He looked helplessly at the unconscious Abby by his feet. 'Will she be all right?'

'She'll have a nasty headache, but she'll be fine,' Stephen said briskly. Although he knew Connor didn't mean to hurt Abby, he was like an annoying little brother. But surely even annoying little brothers wouldn't go around shooting people with tranquillizer darts!

'She better come round soon,' mused Cutter. 'One Raptor was a problem. Two means we've got an infestation. God knows how many are running around out there. I'm going to need all of you to get the Raptors back alive.'

'Alive?' Connor spluttered, momentarily forgetting the professor's rule about returning all creatures to their proper place in time. He shrugged as Stephen frowned at him. 'They're trying to turn us into sushi and we have to play nice. Doesn't seem fair somehow.'

With Connor carrying Abby, the four of them headed back to the locker room to collect the Raptor Connor had knocked out with the tranquillizer dart. Cutter wanted all the dinosaurs back down in the bowling alley so they could be sent back through the anomaly. But as they pushed open the door, Connor immediately realized something was terribly wrong.

The cleaner was missing.

CHAPTER 7

Cutter and Stephen placed the bound giant Raptor as carefully as they could on to a sheet they'd got from the bedding section of the department store. They'd figured this was the only way they'd be able to move something this large down to the anomaly at the bowling alley.

But as they passed through the hi-fi section, Cutter noticed something unusual. All the radios were tuned to the same spot on the dial and were emitting a strange pulsating noise. It was like a regular pattern of interference coming through the radio waves. Cutter wondered if the magnetic field of the anomaly had anything to do with it. As the team's electronics wiz, he'd have to get Connor to look into it.

It wasn't long before they had the Raptors lying in Lane One and ready to send back. Cutter was looking at the stirring baby Raptor thoughtfully.

'It's coming round,' noticed Stephen, readying his gun. 'I'll put it under again.'

41

'Wait,' said Cutter, shaking his head and realizing there might be an easier way to check whether more than two Raptors had escaped from the anomaly. 'One Raptor's an infant. Chances are they're a family unit. Maybe we don't have to go looking for Daddy – maybe junior will bring him here for us.'

The baby Raptor began to stir, thrashing wildly at the rope Stephen had used to secure it to the gutter running down the side of the laneway. For a creature so small, it certainly was vicious. Cutter wondered how on earth the cleaner had managed to survive – with no trails of blood or further evidence of attack, they figured he'd been well enough to leave the mall on his own. From Connor's description of his injuries, perhaps he'd taken himself to the hospital for treatment.

It wasn't long before the distressed cries of the baby Raptor confirmed Cutter's suspicions. While Abby dozed happily on a seat beside the electronic ball return chute, Cutter, Connor and Stephen hid behind racks of sports equipment, watching as an ominous shadow passed by the windows of the bowling alley. Seconds later, the terrifying figure of an adult male Utahraptor came into view in the doorway.

It was at least a metre longer than the other adult Raptor they'd captured earlier. Everything about its size was multiplied tenfold – its teeth, its muscular hind legs, its tail and *especially* its claws. Stephen could see a pair of yellow eyes glinting malevolently in the bowling alley. He was already wondering whether the dosage of tranquillizers they were carrying was enough to knock this one out.

The baby continued its high-pitched shrieks, furiously trying to escape its binding as the adult Utahraptor finally drew up beside it.

They flinched as they realized why the infant Raptor was so distressed. Standing over the smaller creature, the giant Utahraptor sliced through the rope with its claws, and with a single movement tossed the baby into the air. The dinosaur caught the infant in its mighty jaws and began to eat its prey.

'Oh,' whispered Connor, wincing. 'Probably not related, then?'

But things were about to take a turn for the worse. While everyone was paying attention to the drama unfolding on the other side of the bowling alley, Abby had begun to stir. With her eyes half closed, she yawned, standing up groggily.

'What's going on?' she said loudly, as Connor, Cutter, Stephen and the adult Utahraptor turned to look at her simultaneously.

Abby's face fell as she saw the massive creature. It had obviously just made a fresh kill. And Abby could tell from the look in its eyes that she was next on the menu.

Connor ran across the bowling alley as Stephen and Cutter fired at the Raptor. It was already moving towards Abby, and Connor had to sprint to get ahead of it. He grabbed Abby's hand and pulled her out of the way just as a dart lodged in the creature's shoulder.

But it wasn't enough to slow it down. The two friends bolted across the room, wondering if anything could stop it.

Just as they thought it was finally the end for both of them, a most curious thing happened. The Raptor suddenly stopped dead in its tracks, seemingly losing interest in them. Hearing silence behind them, Abby and Connor turned round to be confronted with one of the strangest things they'd ever seen.

The angry Raptor was pacing around, seemingly mesmerized by the slushie machine, churning its lurid blue ice confection. As the machine hummed quietly, the Raptor's electric blue crest fanned open. While Abby and Connor watched in amazement, the incensed creature let forth a ferocious snarl and attacked the glass, smashing it to pieces. Blue ice spewed out across the counter as the carnivore let out a cry of victory.

As Stephen managed to hit the Raptor with a second dart, the dinosaur roared angrily and took off out of the doorway, back into the shopping centre.

'Look at the colour of his crest!' Cutter cried. 'He must have identified the slushies as a threat!'

'You can see his point,' laughed Connor, as Abby stood, dazed, by his side. 'Think of the additives in those things!'

Stephen was the only one not willing to see the funny side of things. He'd had it with the tranquillizer darts – they obviously weren't working. Without saying a word, he furiously threw down the gun and, ignoring Cutter's earlier warning, headed out to the car park. He was determined to get hold of a more useful weapon.

Cutter chased after him, catching up as Stephen reached their truck parked outside. Stephen was in no mood to compromise. For goodness' sake – Abby and Connor had almost been killed!

'These creatures are too dangerous,' he said firmly. 'We can't keep taking stupid risks.'

'Everything we do has an impact,' Cutter urged.

Stephen's reply was curt. 'We've killed creatures before and nothing happened,' he said, unlocking a box in the back of the truck and pulling out a rifle. He frowned as Cutter looked at him uncertainly. 'Look,' the younger man added, trying to be sympathetic, 'maybe the strain of going through the anomalies had got to you. Maybe you only *think* these changes took place . . .'

Cutter stepped back in shock. Stephen had always backed him up and trusted his judgement before. And now here he was, making his own rules and telling Cutter he was delusional?

'You think I dreamt Claudia Brown?' the professor couldn't help laughing.

'The whole pattern of evolution changed but just one person disappeared?' Stephen replied, not answering the question directly. 'One person who happened to be a friend of yours?'

'It's not that simple,' Cutter began. How could he explain this to Stephen and make him believe it? 'The ARC didn't even *exist* when I left. There's a whole team of people there I've never met. There could be countless other things, big and small. I don't know yet –'

Stephen looked at him, not knowing quite how to respond. He knew Cutter had always seen him as an ally, but after the business with Helen he wasn't sure what Cutter thought any more. And since coming out of the anomaly he just didn't seem himself.

'Look,' Stephen said finally, closing the boot of the truck and indicating the rifle in his hand. 'I'll only use this if I have to.'

However, Cutter wasn't finished with the conversation. As grateful as he was for Connor's earlier pledge of support, he desperately wanted Stephen to believe him.

'Who knows what we did wrong back there in the Permian, but whatever it was, we somehow allowed evolution to take a different turn,' Cutter said, trying to match his assistant's stride.

Stephen turned to look at him, a mixture of confusion and annoyance etched on his face.

'I don't *feel* any different,' he sighed. 'I've got the same life I always had.'

'You might feel the same,' Cutter continued, wondering which tack to take, 'but believe me, there was another version of the world once.'

'In my opinion, evolution can stand a little interference,' Stephen challenged.

Cutter rose to the bait.

'You want to play Russian roulette with our future?' the professor said, raising his voice. 'Go ahead! But don't expect me to help you!'

Stephen couldn't stop himself from scowling. Maybe Lester was right. Maybe Cutter did have amnesia. Whatever it was, it was beginning to get quite tiresome now. What's more, it was beginning to interfere with his job.

CHAPTER 8

Cutter, Abby, Connor and Stephen looked down at the two giant Utahraptors, bound together on the bowling alley floor. Once they had the dosage right, it hadn't taken long to bring the second one down after all.

Now, as they marvelled at the prone dinosaurs, Cutter made it clear he was going to return the Utahraptors through the anomaly himself. But he had some unfinished business in the shopping centre first.

Taking Connor with him, Cutter headed up to the hi-fi section of the department store. The radios were still pulsing with interference. Instructing Connor to tune all the stereos to the same frequency, the professor's face lit up as he recognized an old S Club 7 tune playing on the radio.

'Doesn't that seem strange to you?' Cutter asked, a smile spreading across his face.

Connor began to shake his head, unable to figure

49

out why interference would mean anything unusual. Unless . . .

'You think it had something to do with the anomaly?' he figured excitedly, before checking himself. 'Probably just a technical problem at the radio station.'

'Get on to them and find out,' Cutter suggested.

But a light bulb had suddenly flicked on inside Connor's head.

'If it *is* the anomaly,' he stammered. 'It could mean there's radio interference on this wavelength whenever one opens –'

'Which would explain why Helen was always one step ahead of us,' Cutter grinned, finishing off his student's sentence. 'She must be using some kind of short-wave receiver to spot them.'

'We could build our own detector!' Connor added, happy to see Cutter nod in agreement. 'Something that traces an anomaly within seconds of it appearing.'

'If the interference stops when the anomaly disappears, then maybe we're on to something,' Cutter said, suddenly growing serious. The Raptors had to be returned through the anomaly, no matter what. 'If I don't make it back this time, it's down to you.'

As Cutter kitted himself up with weapons and

prepared to go into the anomaly a short time later, Abby took the opportunity to voice her concerns to the professor.

'You really think this is worth the risk?' she asked, as he slung a tranquillizer gun over his shoulder. Cutter just shrugged. 'Something in our lives could change because we kill an animal that doesn't belong here?' Abby continued, pressing him for an answer.

'Ninety-nine times out of a hundred, probably not,' Cutter replied cautiously, keen to avoid a repeat of his argument with Stephen in the car park. Abby was probably the easiest member of the team to get along with, and Cutter needed all the supporters he could get right now. 'But even if there's one small risk, I don't want to take it.'

Abby bit her lip uncertainly. She understood the importance of defending members of the animal kingdom more than anyone. And Cutter had always been protective of the creatures that came out of the anomalies. But his behaviour since he returned to the Forest of Dean had seriously rattled her.

Cutter read her thoughts. At least she should know she wasn't alone.

'Stephen thinks I'm crazy,' he added helpfully.

'He might be right,' Abby smiled, before curiosity

got the better of her. 'This Claudia Brown – what was she like?'

'Does it matter?' Cutter shrugged, wondering whether talking about Claudia was just going to make life more difficult for him in the long run. But something about Abby's expression made Cutter want to open up. She seemed genuinely interested.

'She was OK,' he began, picturing Claudia's pretty face and feeling a stab of pain as he wondered if he was ever going to see her again. 'Loyal, good at her job, a team player. Not as tough as she pretended to be, but strong when it mattered.'

'She meant a lot to you,' Abby said, looking him straight in the eye.

Cutter hesitated, not knowing what to say. He and Claudia had just figured out where they stood with each other when she disappeared. He couldn't deny they had strong feelings for each other.

'Yes,' he said simply.

'I'm sorry that I didn't know her,' Abby replied sadly. 'And that you lost her.' She glanced at the professor, and was startled to see him terribly upset.

The young zoologist felt completely bewildered. Cutter talked about this Claudia girl as if she was so . . . *real*. He was a difficult person to read at the best of times, but he certainly wasn't an actor. It wouldn't be easy for a man like him to fake something like this.

'I want to believe you,' Abby continued, looking down at her feet. 'I really do. But it's just so *hard*.'

'I know,' Cutter said, smiling reassuringly. The fact that Abby was curious enough even to ask about Claudia was enough for him at the moment.

Anyway, they didn't have any more time to talk. Somehow, they had to get the adult Raptors back through to the Cretaceous era before they woke up and the anomaly closed.

CHAPTER 9

Cutter stood up and brushed himself off, checking the two Raptors beside him. They both appeared to have survived the drop OK.

Cutter looked back up behind him. Just moments ago, Stephen and Connor had helped him push the dinosaurs through into the Cretaceous era, and then he'd gone through himself. But he hadn't been expecting the atmospheric rip to be sitting on top of a hillside. Losing his footing on loose rock as he emerged, Cutter had tumbled head first, gathering scratches and bruises along the way.

Cutting the bonds of the dozing Raptors, Cutter turned to make the treacherous climb back up the hillside. With the dinosaurs still unconscious, he took the chance to get his bearings. From his vantage point on the hill, he could see a landscape dotted with huge forests – giant conifer and ginkgo trees towered over cycad ferns. Small, stony hillsides, like the one he was on, were scattered in between them. He'd travelled back over 125 million years, and the view was breathtaking.

Cutter sighed as a majestic winged reptile soared above him. It reminded him of a Pteranodon. The first time he'd seen one, it had been flying over a golf course in the south of London. The creature had come through an aerial anomaly, and Cutter smiled as he remembered that Claudia had, at first, been terrified of it. The Pteranodon had even knocked her out with its powerful beak. But when the time had come to return it, she'd been as amazed by its beauty as he was.

Cutter looked up at the anomaly on the hillside above him. Just as Connor had predicted, its bright light was growing weaker, and Cutter knew it wouldn't be long before it ceased to exist at all. But thinking about Claudia had set his mind in motion. What if he was to stay here? There had to be some way to find her. Maybe he could just stay in the past until he could figure out how to fix the present.

'I thought you might try something like this,' a voice said loudly, tearing into his thoughts.

Cutter spun round, shocked to find Stephen standing behind him.

'That's why I followed you through,' the lab technician added, proving just how well he'd come to know the professor over the years. 'Just in case you had some crazy idea about not coming back.'

'I don't know what you're talking about,' Cutter said, shrugging unconvincingly. He wasn't surprised when Stephen sighed and raised an eyebrow. He'd never been any good at lying. 'Well? So what?' he continued, becoming upset. 'Maybe it's for the best.'

'What?' Stephen replied, trying not to lose his cool. He might think Cutter wasn't his usual self these days, but there was no way he was going to leave him here to be eaten by hungry Raptors. 'Dying out here in this godforsaken place, millions of years away from everything you know?'

'But that's just it!' Cutter cried, clearly frustrated. 'I don't *know* your world any more.'

'And what if there is no way back?' Stephen reasoned. 'What if this world is the only one there is? It's suicide!'

'I don't want to die, Stephen,' the professor said matter-of-factly. 'I just want to make things right again.'

Stephen finally lost his patience. 'Right now, that world back there is the only one there is!' he exploded.

'And you've still got a job to do. So the real question is, are you going to do it or not?'

Stephen turned towards the fading anomaly. Cutter's heart sank. He was right – they were still a team. If Cutter stayed here, then Lester could do whatever he liked with the creatures that came through the anomalies. And then they'd have a lot more problems than just one person going missing.

'OK,' he heard himself say reluctantly. But as Stephen reached out to give Cutter a hand up the rocky hillside, his eyes widened in terror. Cutter followed his gaze to see the giant Utahraptor staggering to its feet, finally waking up from the tranquillizer dose. As the two men turned to scramble up the steep slope, the creature was right behind them, snapping furiously at their heels with its razor-sharp teeth.

As they reached the light at the top, Stephen pushed Cutter through, the anomaly glimmering weakly. As Abby and Connor pulled the professor out into the bowling alley on the other side, the light began to fade.

'Where's Stephen?' Abby shouted urgently, just as Stephen's head appeared through the shivering glow. Cutter and Connor grabbed hold of his arm, but it was clear they were in a prehistoric tug of war – the

Utahraptor had caught up with Stephen and was pulling him back from the other side.

As Cutter threw his arms round Stephen's waist, Connor was horrified to see the anomaly continuing to grow weaker. It almost seemed like Stephen was becoming a ghost before their very eyes. His face and body were fading along with the pulses in the anomaly. As he desperately kicked at the creature, it clamped on to his leg and Stephen cried out in pain.

With his last reserve of energy, Stephen twisted round and reached back into the Cretaceous era. Grabbing a rock, he smashed it into the face of the angry carnivore. The Raptor reeled back in shock as Cutter finally managed to pull Stephen through the light to safety.

But it wasn't over yet. The team watched in dismay as the snapping head of the enraged creature appeared once again through the anomaly. When the Raptor was only halfway into the bowling alley, the light glimmered and froze for a second before disappearing completely. As the dinosaur let out a forlorn shriek, its head and shoulders fell with a thump to the polished wood floor. The rest of its body was lost back in the Cretaceous era, where it belonged.

Stephen looked at Cutter gratefully. There was no need to say anything. They both knew they owed each other. But what on earth were they going to do with half a Raptor?

The next day, Abby, Cutter, Stephen and Connor stood in an ARC office, called in by Lester to wrap up the events of the latest anomaly and meet a new member of the team.

'Some sort of PR wizard,' Lester had said on the phone the night before. 'Basically, he'll be our cover-up specialist, protecting the public from what they don't need to know.'

Cutter had agreed wearily. By that stage he'd been so exhausted and so confused by the events of the day that he would have agreed to just about anything.

As it happened, the new team member wasn't a he, but a she. As the team crowded into the room, the smartly dressed woman sat in a dark corner. But Cutter didn't even glance at her. He was too busy riling Lester.

'You're late,' the government official barked.

'So fire me,' Cutter replied coolly, taking a chair and fixing his eyes on the floor.

'We can only dream,' Lester said, forcing a smile.

'Anyway, now that you're finally here, I'd like you all to meet your new colleague.'

Cutter sighed, resigned to the fact that Lester hadn't even bothered to consult with them about bringing in someone to handle the media. No one understood the situation better than the four people on his team. Whoever this woman was, she probably wasn't going to believe dinosaurs were travelling into the modern day anyway.

The professor finally looked up as the woman came out of her corner into the light.

Cutter couldn't believe what he saw. The same brown eyes, the same slight figure, the same long, perfectly styled brown hair.

It was Claudia.

'This is Jennifer Lewis,' Lester trumpeted, puffing out his chest and running a hand through his hair. He'd been dubious when Leek had said it was a woman, but as Lester ran an eye over her perfectly pressed suit, he couldn't help but be impressed. The girl had class.

But Cutter was dumbfounded. His mind was racing. Looking over at Connor, Abby and Stephen, it was obvious from their muted reaction that they'd never seen her before.

Cutter's mind spun as the woman walked over to greet him, holding out her hand.

'Jenny,' she said, smiling nicely. 'Pleased to meet you.'

He stared at her dumbly. It was clear that as far as Jennifer Lewis was concerned, she had never seen him before either.

CHAPTER 10

Cutter tried to compose himself as Lester continued talking. His air of superiority was infuriating – it was obvious he was trying hard to impress Jennifer.

'Ms Lewis has been appointed to a senior position in the team,' he said. 'That means she answers to me, and you lot answer to her.'

'I didn't know we answered to *anybody*,' Stephen glowered.

Lester straightened his tie and smiled winningly at his star recruit.

'Scientists, Ms Lewis,' he apologized, as if sharing a private joke.

'It's quite all right, James,' the woman replied, smiling at him flirtatiously. 'I'm used to working with creative people. And do call me Jenny.'

It was too much for Cutter. He'd watched the exchange with disgust. The sight of creepy James Lester making eyes at Claudia, or Jenny, or *whoever* she was, was just too much. He had to put a stop to it.

Without thinking, Cutter stepped forward and grabbed the startled Jenny by both arms.

'Claudia!'

The woman was clearly taken aback. 'My name's not Claudia.'

'You're *Claudia Brown*,' Cutter repeated slowly. Jenny grimaced. This strange man was beginning to make her seriously nervous.

'You must be confusing me with someone else,' she stuttered.

'You only *think* you're Jennifer Lewis,' Cutter insisted, tightening his grip. 'You're really a woman called Claudia Brown.' He searched her eyes desperately, looking for any hint of recognition. How couldn't she know him, after everything they'd gone through? 'You've changed somehow . . . I can explain . . . there's a reason for this . . . there has to be!'

Jenny looked over at Lester, visibly shaken. She tried unsuccessfully to force a smile as the government man intervened.

'Meet Professor Nick Cutter,' he sighed, as if Cutter was an exhibition in a zoo. 'A fascinating case study of the tipping point between inspiration and lunacy.'

'Are you feeling all right, Professor?' added Leek, craning to look over Lester's shoulder.

'Claudia, please!' Cutter persisted, ignoring the comments. 'I know this sounds insane, but you're not who you *think* you are. Just listen to me!'

Connor watched as Jenny finally managed to free herself from the professor's grip and anxiously took a step back. He felt genuinely sorry for Cutter. Whatever was going on, it was obviously very real to him. Lester was just standing on the sidelines smirking at him, as if Cutter really *was* insane.

Connor realized he had to get the palaeontologist out of here before he completely flipped out.

'The anomaly detector, Professor . . .' Connor said, stepping in and making Cutter look him in the eye. 'You said we should discuss it, remember?'

Cutter finally drew his gaze away from Jenny and looked at Connor blankly. For the first time in minutes he was aware of other people in the room and suddenly realized how ridiculous this must look. He followed Connor out to the corridor.

'It's Claudia,' Cutter said quietly, leaning tiredly against a wall.

'I know,' Connor said gently.

Cutter's eyes widened in hope.

'Then why didn't you say something?' he whispered urgently.

'I mean, I know that's what you *believe*,' Connor said, furiously backtracking. 'Me? I've never seen her before in my life.'

Cutter shook his head as if trying to dislodge something. It was all too much.

'Listen, Professor, you can't go flaky on us now,' Connor pleaded. 'It's nearly midday already and we'll probably have to save the world again before bedtime.'

Cutter managed a tense smile. He never thought he'd see the day that Connor would be the one talking sense into *him*.

'All right,' he lied. 'I'm OK.'

'No more of this Claudia stuff?' Connor added bravely. Cutter was the one who told him what to do. He couldn't help but feel uneasy when it was the other way around. 'At least until you can work out what's going on?'

Cutter shrugged despondently in agreement. He had no other choice.

After apologizing to Jenny and saying he must have made a mistake, Cutter, along with Leek and Lester, sat down with the ARC's new public relations representative to discuss her role. To say she doubted them when they told her she would be working with real live dinosaurs was an understatement.

'Your job is to come up with convincing cover stories,' Lester added. 'In essence, that means convincing people they didn't see what they actually did.'

By the end of the conversation, Jenny still didn't look like she believed them. Cutter couldn't blame her. As a first day on the job went, so far, this one had been pretty implausible.

CHAPTER 11

Helen Cutter walked slowly through the rocky terrain of the late Cretaceous era. In her mid-thirties, with her long, dark hair pulled back into a ponytail and wearing dark green overalls and a neck scarf, she looked like any other adventurer undertaking an important exploration. Only Helen Cutter wasn't just any other adventurer. And this exploration was taking place in another world, over 75 million years ago.

She'd been walking for a long time. Unlike her usual kempt appearance, she was dirty and looked exhausted. Her attempts to find the future anomaly had so far proved unsuccessful, and she hadn't had a decent meal for ages. She was getting frustrated.

Pulling out a radio transmitter, Helen switched it on, trying to detect any sign of an anomaly. It blinked at her for a second and then flicked itself off. Growing increasingly desperate for a glimpse of the familiar shimmer, Helen scanned her surroundings.

She was surprised to find herself among a small outcrop of rocks. A large Pteranodon nest was built in the middle. With relief, she spied two large eggs sitting unattended inside it. Moving swiftly, she jumped into the ragged mass of twigs and brushwood and placed both of them inside her sturdy rucksack.

Her heart skipped a beat as an ominous shadow flew over her. Letting out a furious squawk at the intruder in its nest, a massive adult Pteranodon swooped towards her. As she crouched down, one of its fierce talons tore through the leg of her overalls. Helen pulled out a large hunting knife from her belt, watching the creature circle and dive down towards her once again.

But Helen was too fast for it, stabbing the Pteranodon deeply in the stomach as it swooped just metres above her. Shrieking in protest, the dinosaur clawed at her again before flying off into the huge forests.

Pulling out a first-aid kit, Helen ripped the material on her overalls and prepared to dress the wound. But suddenly, another thought occurred to her. With a look of stubborn determination, Helen tossed the kit back into her pack and pulled out her anomaly detector. But she didn't flick it on. Instead, she inspected the small wound the Pteranodon had made and picked up her hunting knife. Crying out in agony, she buried it deep into her leg.

As Helen smeared the blood from the wound over her clothes, her mind ticked over with a fresh plan.

Stephen rejecting her advances in the Forest of Dean had humiliated her. But maybe he could prove to be useful yet.

Back in the present that same day, Abby and Connor ambled through the video store. As usual, they were arguing about the evening's viewing.

'You chose last week, remember?' Connor said, watching Abby pull a face. It was the same kind of look she gave when Rex, her pet Coelurosauravus, left surprise deposits of dinosaur poo around the flat.

'Oh, come on,' Abby huffed, putting her hands on her hips. 'Do you really think I would have chosen *The Texas Chainsaw Massacre*? What about something romantic for a change?'

'My worst nightmare,' Connor replied, rolling his eyes. 'Two hours of stupidly handsome people crying a lot and pretending nobody fancies them.'

Abby continued looking down the aisle as Connor watched her thoughtfully. Even though he knew she had a crush on Stephen, it couldn't hurt to drop a hint or two about how he felt.

'Anyway, these movies are all the same,' he added, flashing her a sly grin. 'The heroine spends the whole time chasing some handsome creep then finally realizes she's been in love with her wacky but lovable best friend all along.'

Abby spun round so that the two of them were face to face. She knew *exactly* what game Connor was playing. He had been playing the same one since he arrived at her front door over two months ago, looking for a place to stay. And she wasn't in the mood for it.

'I see your point,' she said, smiling sweetly. 'I mean, that's not going to happen in real life, is it?' Connor's face fell, but Abby continued. 'I'm going home. You choose. But no horror, no action and *definitely* no kung fu.'

Connor felt a lump rise in his throat as he wandered over to the horror section. So that was that. Stephen had broken Abby's heart with his affair with Helen, all those years ago. Connor thought how unfair things were that she didn't realize what a good guy *he* was and come running straight into his arms. All Connor wanted to do was to protect Abby and look after her.

Connor sighed as he picked up a movie from the

rack, smiling appreciatively at the suitably gory picture on the front cover.

'A classic,' said a female voice appreciatively. 'Good choice!'

Connor turned round to be confronted by the most gorgeous woman he'd ever seen. She looked around the same age as him, but their style was worlds apart. While Connor looked like he'd just raided the local charity shop, the girl in front of him was fashionably dressed and had perfectly applied makeup. And she was smiling. At *him*.

'I'm not really in the mood for horror tonight,' she continued, running a perfectly manicured finger along the top of the rack. 'I feel like something a bit more . . .'

'Romantic?' Connor said, pre-empting the remainder of her sentence.

'*Fantasy*,' the girl corrected, smiling wistfully. 'Sci-fi. Something like that. You couldn't recommend anything, could you?'

Connor was unable to hide a stupid grin from spreading across his face. Could he recommend a film to the most gorgeous woman in the world? Could he ever! Abby momentarily forgotten, he scuttled around to Sci-fi.

CHAPTER 12

Cutter was at the ARC, trying to explain to Lester and Leek the discovery he and Connor had made at the department store. They were in Lester's glass-walled office, overlooking the operations centre. As always, Lester was less than enthusiastic.

'It's like tracking down a pirate radio station,' Cutter explained. 'All we need is access to the AMS network and a map and we can triangulate the interference to within 30 metres or so. We can also design a hand-held anomaly detector for use over short distances.'

'So we'll be able to spot the anomalies as soon as they open?' Leek frowned.

'That's the idea,' Cutter nodded.

'Will it be expensive?' Lester scowled. He didn't understand anything about AMS networks and odd-shaped interference hoosy-whatsits. This was just another hare-brained Nick Cutter idea to add to the list, as far as he was concerned.

'Only if we do it *properly*,' Cutter shot back.

'I think this is something we should consider, sir,' Leek cut in suddenly. 'It would be our most significant breakthrough to date.'

Lester looked at his younger charge, intrigued. There was something about the way he suggested the discovery would be attributed to ARC and not this raving Scotsman that he liked. A lot.

'Fine,' Lester finally huffed. 'Tell Leek what you need and he'll see to it.'

'I want Connor to supervise the work,' Cutter added cautiously, suspecting they were up to something.

'*All right!*' groaned Lester, wanting to get the professor off his back. 'But he reports to Leek.' The government man expected Cutter to reply but the palaeontologist seemed to be lost in thought, looking out of the glass window into the main office. Lester followed his line of sight to see Jenny typing a report at the main desk. He rolled his eyes. Cutter was really so predictable these days.

Knowing how much it would annoy the professor, Lester closed the meeting and headed over to chat to the pretty PR recruit.

Cutter watched them flirting with annoyance. Lester was married – a fact the government man often

73

seemed to forget. But as Cutter walked over to try and talk to them, Leek came running into the office, waving something in his hand.

'Reports coming in from the city,' he said breathlessly. 'Looks like a new anomaly!'

Lester ran an eye over the words in front of him, scowling.

'It's a fire,' he said, annoyed his lively repertoire with Jenny had been interrupted. 'Nothing to do with us.'

'We've intercepted mobile calls from inside the building,' Leek replied. 'There's a lot of chatter about foul-smelling gas and a possible creature sighting.'

'C-creature?' Jenny stuttered, her voice rising. She was still convinced the whole dinosaur thing had been a joke. She quickly scanned the ceiling for a camera, wondering if she was being set up for a TV comedy show.

Flicking her hair over her shoulders, Jenny fixed the three men with a gorgeous smile. She'd have to play along with them for now. It wouldn't look good on national telly if she came across as a killjoy.

Across the river, Abby was having some fun with a creature of her own. Her pet dinosaur, Rex, was skipping excitedly around the dinner table of her flat, his bright green crest rising and falling as he fluttered his long, transparent wings. Abby was feeding him mashed-up chicken guts, and this was his favourite part of the day.

They both looked up as the front door of the apartment flew open. Abby frowned as Connor stumbled in, followed by an elegantly dressed woman. In high heels and with her back straight as a pin, there was something about her that Abby disliked immediately.

'Abby, this is Caroline,' Connor babbled, looking like an excited schoolboy.

'Hi,' said Abby, open-mouthed. She'd only left Connor at the video store half an hour ago. And he'd managed to meet a *girl*?

'Nice place,' Caroline said in return, casting a critical eye over the lizard tanks and cactus plants dotted around the room. She let out a frightened squeal when she spotted the bright green Coelurosauravus staring solemnly at her from the table. Rex chirped at her.

'What *is* that thing?' Caroline said hysterically, levelling a long, pointy finger at the little dinosaur.

'That *thing* is a lizard,' Abby replied curtly, disliking the woman more by the minute.

'It's just Rex,' smiled Connor, desperate to please. 'He's harmless. Touch him. Go on.'

Caroline cringed as she put a manicured finger out to stroke Rex on the head. But before she could, the tiny creature flicked out his long, brown tongue and hissed at her. Caroline jumped and backed away, startled.

'Sorry,' laughed Connor nervously. Rex had *never* done that before, to anyone. 'Bad Rex! Bad lizard!'

'He's just doing what his instinct dictates,' said Abby defensively. She picked up the dinosaur and popped him back in the tank that doubled as his home.

Caroline pulled a face as Rex licked Abby's hand.

'I invited Caroline round to watch a DVD,' said Connor, trying to change the subject and pulling out a film with robots on the cover. 'You don't mind, do you?'

'Umm ... no problem,' Abby lied, a bit put out. There was something strange about this woman. Abby couldn't quite put her finger on it.

'Connor and I were having such a good time,' Caroline added, flashing Abby a big smile. 'He's *so* funny, isn't he?'

'Oh, hilarious,' said Abby sarcastically. 'I'm going to put on some tea.'

Cutter was having the worst day of his life.

Abby and Stephen both wondered what had got into the professor.

The vicious Raptors were no match for Cutter and his team.

Although she was terrified, Abby drove the digger to create a distraction.

Stephen knew his friendship with Cutter was
being tested – by Helen.

'Earl Grey for me!' Caroline called out after Abby as she headed towards the kitchen. 'No sugar!'

Unfortunately for Caroline, she never got her tea. Minutes later, Abby and Connor had received news of a new anomaly and were driving furiously towards the ARC on the outskirts of London. Cutter instructed them to pick up some weaponry and come to the location of the new anomaly immediately. Connor was delighted. Caroline had been a bit put out that they'd been called to work, but at least she'd scribbled her phone number on his hand. *Result!*

Abby, on the other hand, was fuming. She revved the engine on her Mini Cooper until Connor's knuckles turned white as he clutched his seat. As far as she was concerned, the girl Connor had met in the video store was *horrible*! And there was something about the way Caroline looked at Rex that really irked her too. She fervently hoped Connor wouldn't ask her round again.

Abby's irritation continued once they'd arrived at the ARC and began picking through the equipment storeroom.

'None of this stuff is any use,' Connor grumbled.

'This is the very latest in high-tech weaponry,' Leek

huffed. He had no idea what any of it was for, but it had certainly been very expensive. 'We've got equipment here that would make James Bond cry with envy.'

'So what?' Connor scowled, picking up a pair of handcuffs. The reports had said there was a possible creature sighting and a noxious gas creeping through the building. What was Leek expecting them to do, lock the gas to a fax machine?

Reading his thoughts, Abby suddenly had a bright idea.

'The garden centre!' she said excitedly. If they could get leaf blowers, they'd be able to lift the smog in a second!

The two of them ran out of the storeroom and headed for the lift. All around them, ARC personnel hurried around the operations centre, preparing reports and keeping an eye on the massive electronic map dominating the lower floor.

But as they sprinted out into the car park, Connor stopped dead in his tracks.

'Hey!' he shouted, calling after a man in an SAS uniform and hat who had just walked past them. The tense soldier turned round. His cap was pulled down low over his eyes as Connor studied him curiously. 'We've met, haven't we?'

'I work here,' the man replied gruffly, pulling his cap down further and shrugging his shoulders. 'You've probably seen me around.'

Connor took a step forward, trying to get a better look. The man backed away, keeping his head lowered and folding up the collar of his jacket. Connor could see ugly, red scars on his neck and jaw. It looked like he'd just gone ten rounds with an angry Raptor or something.

'We haven't got time for this,' Abby said firmly, smiling at the man apologetically and dragging Connor towards the Mini. The soldier walked away briskly, visibly relieved. As they reached the car, Connor stopped, his eyes wide with surprise.

'The scars!' he whispered urgently, pointing back to where the soldier had been standing moments before. 'He was in the mall. The cleaner. That was him!' Abby stared at him blankly as Connor continued. 'He disappeared after the Raptor attack. You *must* remember him.'

'I never really looked at him,' Abby replied, getting into the car. 'And why would one of Lester's soldiers pretend to be a cleaner in a shopping mall?'

Abby had a point. Connor shrugged off his concerns and jumped in the car. Soon, they were too wrapped up in flipping through the *A-Z* to find the nearest garden centre to notice the soldier watching them from a distance.

That was close. First day back on the job after the dinosaur attack and his cover had nearly been blown. He'd have to be more careful next time.

CHAPTER 13

Stephen hurried up the paved walkway towards the multi-storey office block near Tottenham Court Road. Cutter and Jenny were both talking to a fire chief. He'd given the all-clear – there wasn't a fire in the building after all and Jenny had just told him to withdraw the rest of his fighters. But there seemed to be some sort of fog inside the block. And they didn't know where it was coming from.

'Sorry,' said Stephen, as the fire chief left. The younger man was out of breath and looked flustered. 'Got here as soon as I could.'

But Cutter could sense that something was wrong. 'Everything OK?' he asked.

Stephen had to think quickly as he weighed up whether or not to tell the truth. This morning, he'd found Helen, bruised and bleeding, slumped on the steps to his apartment block. He'd brought her inside and helped clean her up. She was still at his place now, recovering from her injuries. But as he'd left the flat, Stephen had told Helen he wanted her gone by the time he got home.

As far as Stephen was concerned, the professor still wasn't back to his normal self. His mind would probably start imagining all sorts of things if he told him what had just happened. He had to make a decision.

'Fine,' the lab technician bluffed. 'Everything's fine.'

Thinking nothing more of it, Cutter shrugged and the two men headed into the front entrance of the building, leaving Jenny outside. It wasn't until they trekked up many flights of stairs that Stephen realized they were doing it the hard way.

'If it's not a fire the lifts will be safe,' he pointed out, panting as he leant against the railing. Cutter nodded. But as they turned to the fire exit ahead, thin trails of mist wafted out from underneath the door. Cutter braced himself as he cautiously opened it.

'What's that?' Stephen shouted, as a dense yellow fog engulfed the stairwell. It definitely wasn't smoke, but the smell was disgusting. 'It's like something's rotting!'

'My guess is it's an ancient version of the Earth's

atmosphere,' Cutter yelled, almost unable to see through the thick cloud. 'Probably Pre-Cambrian, high in sulphur and carbon dioxide.'

Coughing, the two of them made their way into the office.

It wasn't long before Cutter was proved right. An anomaly had opened in the server room on the fifteenth floor, letting through several gargantuan, Pre-Cambrian worms. The carnivorous creatures were thousands of millions of years old, and they were far from friendly. In fact, the worms were over two metres long. And with powerful pink suckers in the place of teeth, they were easily able to attack and kill a grown man.

Once Abby and Connor arrived with the leaf blowers, the slimy monsters didn't stand a chance. The faceless creatures needed the ancient yellow fog to breathe and the air in the present Earth's atmosphere was like poison to them. They were unable to survive once the haze was blasted away.

It was all over in a matter of hours. But the team were all mentally and physically exhausted – and with the added stress of Helen's games, Stephen felt particularly fed up. After fighting Raptors and huge worms, he'd really had enough. How long could they keep on doing this?

'Do you ever wonder if we're doing the right thing here?' Stephen asked his boss, as they'd caught their breath after a run-in with one of the blood-thirsty invertebrates. 'Maybe the anomalies have a purpose. Maybe we should stop fighting and face it.'

'You mean stand by and do nothing?' Cutter was astounded by Stephen's question. It wasn't like Stephen to give up.

'People should know what's happening,' Stephen said, clearly torn. After all this time, he didn't like to think that the team might be doing things the wrong way. 'They need to prepare for what comes next.'

'How do you prepare for a world where evolution has gone mad?' Cutter pointed out. 'We *have* to keep fighting to preserve some kind of natural order.'

As Cutter drove home from the wrap-up at the ARC that evening, he reflected on the conversation with his lab technician. Stephen's behaviour had been a little strange today, especially when he'd arrived at the office block this morning. But maybe it was just the stress of having a new member on the team that was getting to him. He'd come round.

Once again, the professor found himself thinking about the pretty PR representative. Today he'd seen that Jenny could be just as determined about things as Claudia.

Late in the afternoon, at the height of the office block invasion, Jenny had got in on the action. Just like the old Claudia, she demanded to know what was going on and against Cutter's advice, entered the building. Striding out of the lift on the twelfth floor, she'd expected a light mist, but instead ended up helping Cutter kill one of the giant worms!

The professor chuckled as he remembered Jenny's reaction. The horrified look on her face had been priceless – she'd never killed anything, let alone a creature like that, in her *life*. But at least she finally believed the dinosaur part of her job description!

Afterwards, Cutter had been impressed with how well Jenny had handled the fire chief and some office workers who'd seen the giant worm as they escaped the building. She'd convinced them to keep the story out of the press. Claudia couldn't have done it better.

Now, as he drove home, Cutter decided to pay Jenny a visit. He wanted to congratulate her on successfully finishing her first assignment. Driving up an unfamiliar street, Cutter got out of his car as he reached a neat block of flats. It was ARC protocol that all members of the team should have contact details for each other, so Jenny's apartment wasn't so hard to find.

But as Jenny answered the door, Cutter couldn't hide his amazement. She looked so much like *his* Claudia, standing in the doorway, that everything he'd planned to say went right out of the window.

'Suppose there was another world once,' he blurted out before he could stop himself. 'A world where you were another person; suppose there was an accident in the past and that whole world evolved differently. People who once lived were never born, and other people grew up with different lives. What if all that was possible?'

Cutter paused, realizing he'd hardly stopped for breath. He knew it all sounded crazy, but if he could just get her to *believe* him . . .

'Who is it, Jen?' a voice said, coming down the hallway.

Cutter's heart sank as a good-looking man came to the door and wrapped his arms protectively round Jenny.

'You're busy,' Cutter apologized and turned to leave. He didn't need to hear the reply.

Jenny closed her eyes for a few seconds and took a deep breath. She'd caught Cutter staring at her across the office a couple of times, but coming to her flat? It was just a bit too weird. Still, he was vital to the anomaly operation and she didn't want to be responsible for him being thrown off the team. He was obviously troubled. She didn't know whether to feel sorry for him or not.

Confused, Jenny told her boyfriend it was just someone from work, as Cutter slowly walked back down the steps. Behind him, the door clicked shut.

Lost in thought, Cutter headed back to his car. He didn't notice that Helen was in a vehicle on the opposite side of the street, watching him as he drove away.

Helen looked through the windscreen blankly. She'd left Stephen's flat as requested. But that didn't mean she was ready to go back into the Permian era just yet.

CHAPTER 14

Abby shouted from the car window as Connor jumped out of the passenger seat.

'We're going to be late!'

Connor ignored her as he spotted Caroline sitting outside the pavement cafe. He'd promised to meet for coffee, but Cutter had just scheduled the anomaly detector presentation at the ARC. Connor couldn't believe his bad luck.

'Look, I'm really sorry,' he said, tumbling over the guttering and almost landing at Caroline's expensively shod feet. 'I can't stay.'

'That's a pity,' Caroline purred, holding her cheek out as Connor leant in to kiss it. 'Work again?'

Connor looked desperately over at Abby, waving impatiently from the Mini. Why did Cutter need them *now*? Why not in a couple of hours' time? Why, why, *why*? He turned back to Caroline, grimacing.

'I think you must be the busiest student I've ever

met,' Caroline continued, her steely eyes looking at him intently.

'I've really got to run,' Connor stuttered, making no attempt to move. 'You look . . . fantastic, by the way.'

'You're sweet!' Caroline said, brushing her hand across his chin.

'Am I?' replied Connor, utterly transfixed. Leaning down to kiss her beautiful red lips, he was a little taken aback when his new girlfriend moved her face to the side. He only just managed to give her a peck on the cheek. 'I'll text you, ' he added, as his Caroline fluttered her eyelids at him adoringly.

Caroline waved as Connor ran back to the car, flashing him a mouthful of white teeth as he drove off with Abby. But the moment the Mini was out of sight, her smile faded. Flipping open her phone, Caroline scrolled through her photos until a full-body-length shot of Rex came up. She quickly typed in a mobile number, and pressed Send, her expression cool and determined.

Leek was getting impatient. As Abby and Connor screeched into the downstairs car park, Jenny, Cutter and Stephen waited with Leek in his stark ARC office. A giant plasma screen was set up in front of them, displaying complex graphics, radio communication grids and various signals.

'Where's Lester, anyway?' Cutter asked, trying to buy Connor and Abby some time.

'All I can say is that he's engaged on high-level government business,' Leek huffed, trying to sound important.

'In the Maldives?' Stephen asked, picking up a tropical postcard sitting on his desk.

'That's my personal mail!' Leek protested, trying to grab the postcard back. But Stephen was having too much fun. He handed the correspondence to Cutter.

'He doesn't send his love,' the professor said, pretending to pout sadly as he read Lester's scrawl on the back. 'That must be hurtful.'

Cutter grinned as Leek furiously snatched the postcard out of his hands. The boy was so easy to rile it almost took the fun out of it.

At that moment, Connor and Abby arrived breathlessly at the door. Without stopping to say good morning, Connor launched straight into his presentation.

'Meet the Anomaly Detection Device,' he said proudly, acting as if he was addressing an entire auditorium of prospective clients. 'ADD for short.' Connor paused and frowned. He turned to the professor. 'Actually, I think I need a new acronym . . .'

'Connor,' Cutter warned sternly.

'Sorry,' the student answered, looking back at the screen nervously. 'What you're looking at is a fully integrated graphic representation of the radio communications matrix, networking all the UK's transmitters. Keeping watch over the UK twenty-four seven.'

'What's that?' asked Leek, as an alarm sounded and a red light flashed on the map.

'Just a demo,' Connor replied proudly. 'But every time a *real* anomaly appears, this machine will alert us within seconds.' Connor pressed some buttons and the red light flicked off.

Cutter was impressed. He patted the beaming student on the back as Leek's mobile phone started ringing. Cutter watched with interest as Connor pulled out a smaller home-made device from his pocket. About the size of a TV remote control, the contraption was a mass of different-coloured buttons and knobs, with assorted pieces of wire sticking out of the sides.

'This is one I made earlier,' Connor confided, handing it to Cutter. 'A palm-held detector for use in the field. Short-wave radio receiver with an effective range of about one hundred metres.'

'Clever!' the professor said, turning the device round in his hands.

'Have you tried beaming up with it?' Jenny teased.

'This is a serious piece of kit!' Connor gasped, offended. 'Well, it will be when I've ironed out the kinks.'

'Technical question,' Leek suddenly interrupted, finishing his call. 'The detector is online now?'

'Absolutely!' said Connor proudly.

'And it picks up every new anomaly?' Leek continued. Cutter frowned. He didn't like where this was going.

Connor nodded his head uncertainly.

'Then *why*,' trumpeted Leek, pausing for dramatic effect, 'am I being told we've just had a new creature attack?'

Cutter's heart sank as he saw the devastated look on Connor's face. They were both as surprised as each other. A lot was riding on them getting the Anomaly Detection Device right, and Connor didn't make mistakes with his gadgets. But worst of all, there was no way they wanted to be shown up by a creep like Oliver Leek.

CHAPTER 15

Freedom Park was an award-winning amusement complex, nestled among a hundred acres of woodland outside London. It housed a massive water park, adventure sports throughout a vast area of forest and dozens of roller coasters, dodgem cars, ferris wheels and other theme-park rides.

The amusement park's manager, Peter Campbell, was a man who loved his job. Except for today. A creature had just killed a player in the forest paintball field. All Campbell knew about the injuries was that it looked like an attack from some sort of big cat.

Still, Campbell was a professional. He wasn't the kind of person to hide away from his public, and today wasn't going to be any different. Cutter and Jenny found him handing out fun packs and stickers to customers as he walked exuberantly through Sideshow Alley.

He wasn't happy to see them.

'Are you insane? This is peak season!' he hissed, once Cutter had outlined a plan to close down the park until the creature could be found. 'Do you have any idea how much money we're talking about?'

Cutter glowered at him. One of Campbell's visitors had just been mauled to death and all the man was worried about was losing a day of takings? Honestly.

'Hi! I'm Peter!' Campbell suddenly shouted, jogging away from them and slamming a sticker on to the back of an unsuspecting child. 'Hope you're having a great holiday at Freedom Park! Keep smiling!'

'You have to evacuate,' Cutter insisted, as Campbell stepped back.

'He's right, Peter,' said a voice from behind. Cutter and Jenny spun round to see Valerie Irwin standing in front of them. A slender and attractive girl, she looked about the same age as Abby. She was wearing the same garish Freedom Park uniform as Campbell. Her boss growled at her.

'If I want your opinion I'll ask for it!' he spat, tripping over himself to corner another group of visitors. 'Hi! I'm Peter! Keep smiling!'

'We don't want to create unnecessary panic,' Jenny purred reassuringly, avoiding eye contact with Cutter. 'Suppose we close the paintballing area as a precaution and leave everything else open? How does that sound?'

Cutter was shocked by Jenny's compromise. If a prehistoric creature was on the loose, how could they guarantee containment in that one small area of forest! What was she thinking? But before he could respond, Campbell and Jenny were shaking hands.

'I can live with that,' the manager said as he plastered a sticker across the forehead of a passing grandmother. 'Keep smiling!' Campbell turned to Jenny grimly. 'And if you say the words "big cat" out loud, I'll sue you.'

Fuming, Cutter followed Jenny as she walked briskly through the park. He wanted an explanation.

'Evacuate and we'll have media meltdown,' Jenny replied simply. 'How am I supposed to keep a lid on that? What if the press stumble over an anomaly in the woods?'

Maybe she had a point. Cutter grimaced as they walked past the roller coaster and the screams of excited children filled the park. At least the noise should keep the creature away. No predator on Earth would want to be around that racket.

Even so, the professor was worried. Something just didn't sit right about this whole thing. Connor had checked his equipment and was one hundred per cent certain that the anomaly detector was working perfectly. But a quick scan of the forest as they came through had come up with nothing – there were no familiar circles of light glimmering anywhere.

When the team had inspected the body of the dead paintballer, Abby had been sure the lethal claw marks pointed to an attack by a large cat, as big as a lion. Surely if something like that was roaming around, they would have seen it by now – not to mention the anomaly it had come through.

Cutter was distracted by his mobile ringing. It was Stephen.

'I've picked up a trail,' he said, as Cutter quickened his pace. 'About a mile west of the paintballing area, near the main gate.'

Out in a remote part of the forest, Stephen was crouching in a clearing, inspecting a large imprint in the mud. Above him, a rope bridge with a thin, wooden plank for a walkway swung in the breeze. It was strung between two trees as part of the aerial assault course of the adventure sports playground.

Stephen realized Abby had been right – the evidence in the wet dirt certainly *looked* like it belonged to some type of giant cat. The depth of the footprint proved it was a heavy creature, probably weighing up to two hundred kilograms. No modern-day cat could make an impact that big.

Bells rang way off in the distance as joyful holidaymakers rode through the forest on bicycles. At the same time, Stephen's phone beeped to indicate he'd got a text message. He flipped his phone open, rattled to see a picture of Helen fill the screen.

'*I'm fine now, thanks to you,*' the message read. '*You're the best. See you, love Helen.*'

'Everything OK?' Cutter said, arriving in the clearing with Connor in tow. Stephen looked as white as a sheet.

'Fine . . . it's nothing,' Stephen stammered, looking quickly at the photo again before pressing Delete. He still wasn't intending to tell Cutter about what had happened yesterday. But he had made it pretty clear to Helen not to contact him again. Why was she making things so difficult?

Shrugging his shoulders, Cutter outlined their next move. As far as he was concerned, if the creature had killed once, it was bound to strike again. And if it was prehistoric as he suspected, then it was more than likely a Smilodon, a giant sabre-toothed cat from the late Pleistocene era. Given the forests it would have

97

lived in during that period, the creature would be comfortable with woodlands like this and able to hide itself well.

They had to be careful using tranquillizer guns in a public place like Freedom Park, though. So whatever this creature was, they were going to have to trap it.

Right on cue, a bright yellow digger thundered into the clearing. Abby jumped down from the machine's cage, smiling at Connor as she brushed dirt off her baggy canvas trousers. She knew he was grumpy. Once again he'd been denied a tranquillizer gun, and now she got to drive the big trucks as well! She couldn't help stifling a giggle.

'If we dig a second trap here we've got the whole area covered,' Stephen said, pointing at an area on the map Cutter had just pulled out of his rucksack.

Taking Connor with him, Stephen left the clearing and walked off into the surrounding woods. Jumping back into the digger, Abby immediately set to work.

As the machine burrowed a deep trench in the forest floor, Cutter began collecting branches and leaves. He then pulled chunks of fresh meat from a bag in his rucksack, placing them carefully on top of the foliage to attract the Smilodon. But as the arm of the digger pulled back a fresh mound of dirt, Cutter's eyes widened.

'*Stop!*' he shouted urgently, waving his arms at Abby. '*Stop digging!*'

Abby turned the engine off curiously and got out. Cutter had already leapt down to the bottom of the pit and was inspecting what the digger had just uncovered. As she crouched down to see, Abby gagged. Sticking out of the dirt was a human hand.

But before she could say anything, a deafening roar broke out from the forest behind them. Gulping, Abby turned round, unable to believe what she was seeing. She'd dealt with plenty of big cats in the zoo, but nothing quite like this.

An adult sabre-tooth had sprung into the clearing, two massive eighteen-centimetre-long fangs protruding from the top of its mouth. Spotting its prey, the creature let out a furious snarl. Unlike the lions and tigers Abby was used to, this fearsome cat had a body more like that of a large bear, rather than a feline.

With its huge bulk and thick neck, it looked completely terrifying. And Abby had no desire to become better acquainted.

CHAPTER 16

Abby had no time to think. She raced for the digger, hoping the safety cage would be enough to protect her. But the Smilodon seemed to have other ideas. As Abby turned back, she was horrified to see it angrily pacing around the edge of the pit, hungrily swiping at a trapped Cutter with its mighty claws.

Climbing into the cab and switching on the digger, Abby furiously gunned the engine. Her plan for distraction was a success – within seconds the sabre-tooth was hurling itself on to the cab of the vehicle, trying to smash its way through the glass windscreen. Its powerful jaws were just centimetres from Abby's face.

Scrambling out of the pit, Cutter headed for the ladder leading up the tree to the rope bridge. Despite the chaos, for a moment he couldn't help trying to get a clear look at the Smilodon. Their kind had been extinct for over 10,000 years, and Cutter was now getting the chance to see one up close – even if it was a little bit *too* up close. Now, if he could just lure it towards him . . .

Cutter wouldn't have to wait long. Terrified, Abby switched the mechanisms on the safety cage of the digger so that the cab began to spin. Unable to hold on, the creature snarled fiercely as it was thrown off the vehicle, right underneath Cutter.

Without a moment to lose, the palaeontologist ran along the swaying platform. Holding on tightly to a branch and pulling out his hunting knife, he began hacking at the anchor ropes.

Spotting the flurry of activity going on in the treetops above, the agile Smilodon quickly and easily scaled the tree trunk and stepped out on to the flimsy bridge. But as it manoeuvred its considerable weight on top of the wooden plank, Cutter sliced through the final rope. Howling in protest, the massive creature sailed through the air and landed on all fours on the forest floor.

Abby and Cutter exchanged relieved glances as the mighty sabre-tooth let out a defiant, raging roar before disappearing back into the woods.

Seconds later, Stephen and Connor came rushing in from the opposite side of the clearing, drawn by the ruckus they'd heard as they searched the paintball area. They listened in alarm as Abby and Cutter replayed the scene, before pointing out the gruesome find in the trap beside them. Cutter and Stephen jumped in, loosening the dirt around the hand. It wasn't long before they'd uncovered the wounded remains of a young man.

'He was savaged,' said Cutter, grimacing at the violent injuries. It certainly didn't look like they'd been made by a human. 'Virtually cut in half.'

'How long do you think he's been here?' Abby asked, feeling a little woozy.

'A few weeks,' Cutter replied, taking a guess. He was surprised to see Connor's face brighten.

'If the body's been here that long the anomaly could have formed *before* the detector came online!' the student suddenly whooped, delighted. 'There's nothing wrong with it!'

'One problem,' Cutter replied, unable to share Connor's joy. 'The sabre-tooth may have killed this man. But it sure didn't dig a trench six feet deep and bury his body.'

'Someone knows,' Abby said, as the others nodded in agreement. 'They've been protecting it.'

Realizing it was time to do another sweep of the forest, Abby, Connor and Stephen split up and left

Cutter to guard the pit. There was no point in leaving the body here for the prehistoric cat to maul for a second time.

Waiting for the others to come back, Cutter decided he might as well try to identify the unfortunate sabre-tooth casualty. His face fell as he found a wallet in the inside pocket of the hapless victim's leather jacket. There, among a few notes and some credit cards, was a photograph. It was a picture of the man with a young woman who was obviously his girlfriend. With her lurid Freedom Park uniform and slight features, Cutter recognized her immediately. It was Valerie Irwin, the staff member Campbell had snapped at this morning while Jenny and Cutter were trying to get the park evacuated.

Remembering Abby's suggestion that someone was sheltering the creature, Cutter covered the body and sprinted out of the clearing. He headed towards the Freedom Park front office to get Valerie's contact details. The team had to get hold of the sabre-tooth, and Cutter was sure she knew where to find it.

Cutter rang on the doorbell of a small cottage nestled in farmland, not far from Freedom Park. Valerie hadn't arrived at work today. But as Cutter waited impatiently at the front door, it didn't seem like she was at home, either.

The professor walked round the side of the building, making a snap decision to get into the house his own way. Smashing a glass panel with the butt of his tranquillizer gun, he quickly unlocked a window and scrambled through to the kitchen at the back.

The cottage was completely still. Leaving his gun on the kitchen table, Cutter wandered into the neat living room. Looking around, he noticed a framed photograph sitting on a sideboard by the far wall. It was another shot of Valerie and the dead young man they'd found in the forest, smiling happily. Only this time, Valerie was cuddling what looked like a stocky young tiger cub. Even though its trademark fangs were yet to develop, Cutter knew instantly that it was the sabre-tooth as an infant.

The professor pulled out his mobile, urgently calling Stephen's phone number and giving him Valerie's address as he answered. When he'd finished the call, Cutter turned round to retrieve his gun.

But Valerie had got to it before him. Walking quietly into the kitchen while his back was turned, she'd picked up the weapon and was now pointing it straight at him. She was crying.

Cutter took a cautious step forward, holding his hands up to calm her. Valerie's hands shook violently. The front office had called to tell her Cutter had just been there, asking for her address. Valerie knew they'd been digging in the forest. And she had a pretty good idea why Cutter was here now.

'It was an accident,' she stuttered, waving the gun at the professor, warning him not to come closer. 'Dave got careless . . . he didn't know how to handle him.'

Cutter took a deep breath. So *that* was it. Valerie's sabre-tooth pet had killed her boyfriend, and she'd done what she thought was best so the giant cat wouldn't be taken away. She'd acted in a moment of madness and buried the evidence.

'Look, we can sort this out,' Cutter said, his green eyes looking at her intently. 'It's not too late.'

'I was so scared,' Valerie continued, talking to herself more than Cutter. 'I was going to tell the police, but I knew they'd say it was my fault. Everything just happened, I didn't mean any of it . . .' The professor watched anxiously as Valerie tightened her grip on the gun. She was becoming hysterical now, with tears flowing down her cheeks. 'I went into my garage one day and he was just somehow magically there – a tiny cub . . . frightened and alone, half dead. I had to look after him!'

'You did well, Valerie,' Cutter replied calmly, slowly reaching out his hand. 'But you have to give him up now; please, let me help you.'

Both of them flinched as the rifle went off abruptly. A tranquillizer dart whizzed past Cutter's face and buried itself deep into the wall behind him. The young woman looked as shocked as he did.

'I'm sorry,' she stammered, moving around to the door leading to the remainder of the cottage. 'It's too late. I didn't want any of this to happen, but I can't abandon him now. I'm sorry.'

Without saying any more, Valerie pulled on the handle and stepped through the doorway. Cutter was horrified to see the giant figure of the sabre-tooth standing in the hallway. As Valerie led it into the living room, the creature seemed almost playful, flicking its tail from side to side and growling softly.

'He'll kill us both!' Cutter said, unable to take his eyes off the Smilodon's deadly fangs.

'He'd *never* hurt me,' Valerie said confidently, stroking her pet's fur. 'I'm the closest thing to a mother he's ever had.'

Closing the door behind her, Valerie left the room.

Cutter took a step back as the gigantic cat came towards him. Now that its keeper had gone, it was no longer looking so playful.

CHAPTER 17

Letting out a thunderous roar, the sabre-tooth lunged for Cutter as he ran back through to the kitchen.

Grabbing a toaster off the counter, the professor hurled it towards the now furious beast. But the creature just knocked it away with its enormous paw, as if shooing away a fly. As Cutter edged round the bench to move back into the living room, he continued to throw whatever he could get his hands on – first the bread bin, then the electric kettle, then a pot and frying pan from the cooker top. As Cutter passed by the cutlery draw he pulled that out too, sending a barrage of tin and metal flying towards the raging Smilodon. The prehistoric cat snarled in confusion as Cutter saw his chance to escape.

Darting through to the hallway, Cutter headed for the front door. To his horror, it was locked. With no other way out, Cutter's only option was to head up the staircase beside him.

Cutter could hear the monstrous creature padding up the flight of steps as he sprinted into a small bedroom. Slamming the door behind him, he desperately began trying to open the double-glazed windows. His heart sank as he realized they'd been deadlocked. Even when he picked up a chair and threw it at the windows, the strengthened glass stayed firm.

Cutter spun round as the two-hundred-kilogram cat burst into the room, howling as it easily sliced through the flimsy wooden doorway. Thinking on his feet, Cutter grabbed the duvet from Valerie's bed and threw it over the beast. It writhed in confusion, gnashing angrily at the material as feathers flew around the room.

With precious seconds up his sleeve, Cutter headed to the bathroom, relieved to see a small, open window above the toilet. But as he jumped on to the seat, the prehistoric cat appeared, its massive frame taking up the whole of the tiny doorway. Just as it was preparing to leap, Cutter grabbed a can of air freshener sitting by the toilet and sprayed it in the bewildered Smilodon's face.

Cutter took his chance and half leapt, half fell out of the window. He landed with a thud on to the roof of the garage at the back of the house. Jumping into the small walled garden, he was dismayed to see the sabre-tooth crash through the same gap, its massive body bringing down half the upstairs wall with it. The cat deftly landed on the grass just metres away from him and growled menacingly.

Racing over to a collection of tools propped up against a fence, Cutter picked up a garden fork and faced the prehistoric cat as it began slowly pacing towards him. But as the creature flexed its large jaw, it was distracted by shouting from the garden behind them. Cutter turned and was surprised to see Valerie standing on the path.

'Don't hurt him!' she shouted. She quickly moved in between the scientist and the Smilodon.

'Valerie, stay away!' Cutter urged, watching with concern as the young woman took the sabre-tooth's large head in her hands. Her presence seemed to calm it. Valerie was patting it now, as it once again growled softly.

For a moment, Cutter wondered if it could really be more than a harmless kitten. But without warning, a primal urge seemed to overtake the cat as it let out a brutal roar and forcefully wrenched itself away from Valerie's caring embrace. As Valerie screamed, the blood-thirsty carnivore knocked her to the ground, crushing her beneath the weight of its giant paws. Cutter charged at the creature with the fork but, with little effort, the sabre-tooth smacked the garden tool out of his hands. Backing away, Cutter could only look on helplessly as the cat slashed at Valerie's neck with its razor-sharp fangs. The whole horrifying turn of events was over in a matter of seconds. There was nothing Cutter could do to save her.

The sabre-tooth roared as it turned its attention to the professor. With no weapon on hand, Cutter realized he was in big trouble. But as the cat once again moved towards him, a gunshot rang out across the garden. Two darts sailed through the air and landed in the creature. Cutter looked over with relief to see Stephen standing in the gateway, lowering his rifle. The Smilodon looked from one man to the other with confusion as it swayed from side to side.

Seconds later, it collapsed on to the grass, knocked out cold.

It was early evening as Cutter made his way through the harshly lit hallways of the Anomaly Research Centre. He'd organized a debriefing on the sabre-tooth incursion and wanted to check on Connor's detection device.

Cutter pushed unenthusiastically on the glass door leading to the walkway above the main centre. He was still shaken by Valerie's needless death and certainly wasn't looking forward to going ten rounds with Leek.

Cutter found the young government man sitting smugly in his glass-walled office, chatting amicably with Jenny.

'Sadly the creature died while being transported back to the ARC,' Leek announced, smiling unsympathetically as Cutter walked into the room. 'A heart attack, probably induced by shock.'

'I don't understand,' Cutter couldn't help but feel suspicious. He'd seen it loaded safely into the transport truck himself. 'It was a perfectly healthy animal.'

'Perhaps Abby overestimated the tranquillizer dosage,' Leek suggested, his ever-permanent smirk giving nothing away.

Cutter glowered at him. Abby was a highly skilled zoologist – she knew exactly what she was doing. And Leek was well aware of that fact.

'It was out of its time,' Jenny said gently, trying to diffuse the situation. She was sorry for Cutter. It was obvious he felt something for these creatures. 'Maybe it just couldn't cope with the modern world.'

'In the end, isn't it all for the best?' added Leek airily. 'After all, what does one do with a bad tempered sabre-tooth?'

'I want to do my own post-mortem,' Cutter demanded, trying to keep his temper. But Leek just smiled at him arrogantly.

'I'm afraid it's been destroyed,' he replied, ignoring Cutter's astonished look of frustration. 'We have to be aware of the risk of disease. Now, if you'll forgive me, I'm going home. This whole experience has been *totally* exhausting for me.'

Without waiting for an answer, Leek picked up his dark suit jacket and left the room. Cutter watched him angrily, clearly put out. He wished more than ever that Claudia was here – at least she'd understood where he was coming from. She'd stuck up for him more times than he could count. Dealing with Leek was like dealing with a mini-Lester. And both men were equally impossible.

Little did Cutter know that the government official wasn't going straight home after all. Instead, ten minutes later, Oliver Leek was sitting in a deserted car park. He was strumming his fingers impatiently on the steering wheel of his expensive government car.

The person he was waiting for was late. He hated it when people wasted his time.

Leek let out an over-exaggerated sigh when the passenger door finally opened and Caroline got in. As always, her hair was perfectly styled and she reeked of expensive perfume. Leek couldn't help but smile at her appreciatively. She was stunning.

Producing his wallet, he pulled out a large wad of notes. Caroline scowled as he finished counting them.

'It's not enough,' she said, sticking her nose in the air stubbornly.

'It's what we agreed,' Leek replied smoothly as she turned the money over in her carefully manicured hands.

'You haven't got that little creep Connor trying to put his tongue in your mouth,' Caroline spat back.

Leek smiled as she continued frowning at him. Really, it was quite cruel to make a beautiful woman like Caroline pretend to be in love with a sub-human like Connor Temple.

'Sometimes you have to take one for the team,' he shrugged. 'But for what it's worth, you have my sympathy.'

Caroline's expression softened. At least Leek had

some kind bones in his body. After dealing with his cold manner the last few weeks, she was beginning to wonder. Still, this was a small fortune compared to what she'd been making doing other jobs lately.

'He's OK, I suppose,' she said, resigned. They were going out for dinner tonight, and as always, she wasn't looking forward to it.

As Caroline went to open the door, Leek gave his final instruction.

'Stay close to him,' he commanded. 'Find out anything you can.'

Caroline frowned. She knew it all had something to do with the weird lizard in Connor's flat, because Leek had insisted she get a photo. But apart from that, she'd not found anything interesting to report about Connor at all. He liked sci-fi. He believed in aliens. And he had that bad-tempered zoologist as a flatmate. He was just a boring student. Why did the government want information on someone as dull as *him*?

'What's this all about, anyway?' she said finally, unable to hold her curiosity any longer. Leek gave her a steely look. 'None of my business, I get it!' she nodded, stretching her long legs out of the car before looking over her shoulder at him. 'I'll be in touch.'

Leek stared intently at Caroline as she walked over

to her car and drove away. She was right – it *was* none of her business. Leek knew it would be a while yet before he could gather all the information he needed on Nick Cutter, Stephen Hart, Connor Temple and Abby Maitland. But as long as people like Caroline were willing to help him, that's all that mattered.

Leek's thin red lips curled up into a sneer as he started his car and finally headed for home. As far as he was concerned, everything was going according to plan.

Back at the ARC, Cutter looked over at Jenny, who for once was smiling at him kindly. It was obvious that she knew Leek had been lying about the fate of the sabre-tooth.

The two of them made their way down to the main floor of the ARC, stopping in front of Connor as he pulled himself out from underneath the Anomaly Detection Device. The student quickly brushed himself off and went to stand in front of the busy screen, which was once again showing a satellite view of the country and complex radio grids.

'That's it,' he said with a flourish, typing a final code on the keyboard. 'This thing is now officially double and triple checked.'

Connor's eyes lit up as an alarm sounded, beeping while a red dot flashed urgently on the map. He turned to Cutter with his mouth open, unable to say a thing.

'Demonstrations prove nothing, Connor,' Jenny said flatly, oblivious to his excitement.

'It's not a demo,' Connor replied, punching his fist in the air victoriously. 'We've got an anomaly! It works! It actually works!'

'So what are you standing here for?' Cutter pointed out. He couldn't help but smile, imagining the cogs whirring in Connor's brain. The student looked at him in surprise.

'Oh, good point,' Connor exclaimed. But then his face fell. 'But I've got a date with Caroline . . .'

'Cancel it,' Cutter said, making it clear he wasn't giving Connor an option. He punched Stephen's number into his phone to notify him about the new anomaly. 'She'll understand.'

Connor groaned inwardly as he obediently followed Cutter out of the door. Caroline had grown increasingly persistent that they see each other the last few days, and he'd hardly spent any time with her at all. What was the old saying? Absence makes the heart grow fonder. Connor's dour expression changed as he grinned wildly. If he cancelled tonight, then surely she'd be absolutely *dying* to see him the next time! Connor pulled out his phone to call her, walking with a sudden spring in his step.

Beside him, Nick Cutter was smiling too. He could worry about the problems he had with Leek later, but right now, he felt a surge of hope.

All that mattered now was that they were on their way to a new anomaly. Maybe this would be the one that could help them unlock the secrets of time, once and for all.

But more importantly, Cutter had finally found a reason never to give up.

Claudia.

He didn't care how long it would take, or how many worlds he would have to explore. He *would* find her.

After all, he thought as he grinned at Connor fussing over his new machine, now he had time on his side.

PRIMEVAL

Scarily good Primeval books from Ladybird, Puffin and DK.

Packed full of fun and activities, these books are far from prehistoric.